SURVIVOR'S SNIPER

HUNT SECURITY, BOOK 3

JASMINE C. CALDWELL

Contents

Content Warning

The Hunt Security series has an overarching plot and is best read in order.

This series deals with darker themes and may trigger some readers. Trigger warnings: domestic violence, human trafficking, explosion, military injury, PTSD flashbacks, hostage situation

Her world is finally turning around.
His just blew up in his face.

When the syndicate captured Josie, it placed her life on hold. She's lost time that she can never get back. Now safe under Hunt Security's protection, she's desperate to rebuild while she waits for news from the FBI. When Roger asks for a favor, she jumps at the opportunity to repay her rescuers and put her nursing skills to good use.

Finn's life as a sniper is over. He didn't expect to be home for the holidays, but he knows he's lucky he came home at all. What's also unexpected is the beautiful client that's staying with his brother. But when Finn finds out she's going to be his nurse, his resentment surfaces. After coming to an understanding, they start to heal each other.

But when the FBI calls, Josie steps back into danger. Will Finn fall back into the darkness?

Prologue

JOSIE CAREFULLY TIPTOED INTO the apartment. Her book bag was lighter now that she'd sold her textbooks back. She'd finished her RN degree. Graduation was three short days away. She'd have to sit for her boards to get her certification, but the hard part was over.

Bottles around the living room said her boyfriend had been drinking again. Ever since he'd lost his job, it had gotten worse and worse. Never mind that his hangovers had been the reason he got fired in the first place. Now that she was done with school and could start looking for nursing jobs, she'd be able to get away from him. The love had been gone for a long time. She shook her head and started cleaning up like she did every day. Her student stipend was supposed to cover her half of the rent and utilities, with some left over for groceries. Lately she'd had to cover the entire rent and their bills.

How he got the money for all this liquor was beyond her, but he managed to beg it off his buddies somehow. Josie had taken the cash from the bookstore to open her own separate checking account at the bank. When they'd combined finances two years ago, he convinced her it would be better while she was a student to have access to his money. Now all their money was gone. And the last thing she needed was him having access to her future paychecks.

Suggesting he cut back on alcohol so he could get another job hadn't gone well. She'd only brought it up once. Unfortunately, she had no way out until she could get a nursing job.

"You're late," Brad growled from the doorway.

Josie swallowed as she bagged up the trash in the kitchen. "I had to stay to talk to a professor."

"Look at me."

She raised her head and did as he told her to.

"You're lying."

"No, I'm not, Brad." She totally was. She'd gone back to campus after the bank to apply for jobs online using the school computers. Their internet had been shut off ages ago because they didn't have the money to pay the bill. It had been a blessing to have an excuse to hide at school longer. Now that she didn't have any more projects to do, she'd have to get creative.

"You were meeting with that guy from your group project again."

"Don't be silly. He's got a boyfriend."

Brad made a face of disgust. "I don't believe that for a second."

Josie fought not to roll her eyes and added more trash to the bag. It didn't matter what the truth was, he'd never believe her.

As much as she'd hated her parents' strict rules, and the church they'd raised her in, Josie wondered if leaving her old town with Brad had been the right call. At the time, she'd been a desperate twenty-year-old with her eye on the future. The only positive thing to come from this was her degree, even if she hadn't been able to go to a four-year college like she'd wanted to. It was all she could do to get the grants for this program.

Her parents had made it clear she wouldn't be welcome back if she failed. They hadn't approved of her dating a man who didn't go to their church, and they completely disowned her when she moved out to live in sin. So now that she'd made her bed, she'd have to lie in it long enough to get out.

Some of her fellow students at the community college had talked about renting a house. It would be doable with four or five of them. Josie figured she could get out faster if she could find a roommate. So once she passed the NCLEX, the test to get her nursing license, she'd start looking for jobs. Preferably somewhere far away from Nowheresville, Montana.

She'd tried to get away, once. One of the girls who'd been a year ahead of her had invited her to live with her after seeing a bruise on her arm before she could cover it up. But after only one night away, Brad had showed up and dragged her back. She suspected, but he never confirmed, that he'd placed a tracker on her phone. Living in a small town, it would be easy for him to track her down without one. And these community college credits wouldn't transfer just anywhere. So she'd played it off as just an accidental sleepover with a friend after studying too late.

When Gina had graduated and moved away, she'd asked Josie to go with her. But Josie only had one semester left at that point, and she didn't want to start over. They'd kept in touch for a while, Josie always insisting she was fine, but Gina's messages had tapered off when her dad got sick.

Alzheimer's wasn't fun for anyone.

Brad had gone back to watching television on their cheap TV antennae, so she set out to cook dinner. She'd set some chicken in the refrigerator to thaw that morning before her last final exam. As she preheated the oven, she coated the chicken in a tiny bit of melted butter and bread-crumbs. Then she popped it into the pan and covered it with foil. Pulling two potatoes out of the bag, she washed them and pricked holes with a fork before covering them with foil.

Food stamps had been a lifesaver, but they didn't go very far. She had to be very careful about what she bought at the grocery store. The one time she'd asked Brad to pick up stuff from her list, he'd brought home a bunch of junk, and they ran out of money for the month. That was the last time she handed him their EBT card.

With the chicken and the potatoes in the oven, Josie hefted the garbage bag and walked out to the living room. She picked up the beer bottles Brad had left on the coffee table, one of them half full. Holding it out to him, she asked, "Are you going to finish this, or should I dump it?"

"Give me that," he snarled and grabbed it from her hand. Brad went back to ignoring her.

She sighed. Hopefully, one of those jobs would call her, so that all she'd have to do would be to focus on her boards. Tying the bag closed, she stopped by the front door to the apartment. "Brad, this is heavy. Can you take it out during the commercial break?"

"I'm watching the game!"

Groaning inwardly, she carried the bag down three flights of steps, stopping on the landing when she thought it would break. Down to the first floor, and out the back door to the parking lot, where the dumpster sat. Spring was coming to Montana. The sun was setting and the evening breeze cooled her sweaty forehead after she lifted the bag into the dumpster with a grunt. Maybe she should start working out. Josie shook her head. Brad would hate the idea of her going to a gym and he would make her life even more of a living hell. As it was, he mostly left her alone, unless he wanted sex. Thank God for whiskey dick. She hadn't been attracted to him in months. Not since he'd gone down a bottle and hadn't come back up.

Trudging back into her apartment, she checked the timer and saw she had enough time to work on her NCLEX study guide some more. That occupied her time while dinner cooked. She'd gotten used to blocking out Brad's shows while she studied so it didn't faze her. When the timer went off, she jumped up to take out the potatoes and chicken and heated up the frozen peas in the microwave. She made up two plates and set them at the table.

"Brad, dinner's ready!"

"I'll be out in a minute."

Josie waited for a few, but after the steam had died down, she dug in, anyway. She'd learned to eat while their food was still warm.

"Come on, it's getting cold!"

Brad grumbled, but came to the table. She could hear a commercial playing in the background.

"Are we winning?"

He mumbled a reply, but she didn't ask him to repeat himself. She didn't actually care about the game. But it would be nice to feel like friends again, even if they were barely roommates anymore.

Where had the charmer gone? The guy who romanced her and swept her off her feet with talk of white picket fences and beautiful children. At this point, she'd settle for a guy who gave her the time of day.

She'd barely finished dinner when there was a knock at the door. Brad rose from the table like his butt was on fire. "I'll get it."

"Okay." She cleared the table, wiping the plates and putting them in the sink to wash. From where she stood, she caught snippets of Brad's conversation.

"You got the money?"

"She's a pretty one."

Josie turned the sink on, not wanting to think about Brad's jealous streak. She'd once thought it was romantic that he was so possessive of her. Now she saw it for the toxic trait it really was.

She scrubbed and rinsed and set the wet dishes on the drying rack next to the sink. Brad's guest was still here? She turned, wiping her wet hands on the towel she kept on the oven door. "Hi, I'm Brad's girlfriend."

"Not anymore, you're not." The stranger said. Brad stuffed what looked like a wad of cash into his back pocket.

"What is he talking about?" Her blonde brows furrowed in confusion. Why would Brad be breaking up with her—in front of a *stranger*, no less — and why wouldn't he tell her himself?

"You're going with Steve."

"I will not! If you're kicking me out, Brad, I can leave on my own."

"No, you can't. The car's in my name, *sweetheart*." He spat the term of endearment like it was poison. "And besides, he's bought you fair and square."

What in the *world*? "You can't buy a *person*! That's illegal!"

Steve flicked dirt from under his nails and then rummaged in his coat pocket. "You didn't say she was a screamer."

"Never has been before," Brad said as Steve moved toward her.

Her eyes darted back and forth between the two men, neither of which she knew anymore. Josie never cursed, even after leaving her zealous family and community. But this situation called for it. She moved toward the back of the room, away from whatever Steve had in his hand. "What the fuck, Brad?"

"Just go along quietly and nothing bad has to happen."

"Like hell I will!" She started forward, red coloring the edges of her sight as her world narrowed to the man who'd betray her like this. Her pulse pounded in her ears. "You lazy, worthless drunk—" A sharp pain pierced her neck, and everything went dark.

Chapter 1

THE SUMMER SUN BEAT down on him as he pushed the lawnmower into the shed. Finn shut the doors and leaned back against them, lifting his hat to wipe the sweat from his forehead. He took in the two-story farmhouse they'd bought. The red rosebushes they'd planted looked amazing next to the whitewashed porch. His work for the day done, he jogged to the backdoor and slipped inside the kitchen.

His wife stood stirring something at the stove, and it smelled amazing. She'd tied her long hair back while she cooked like she always did.

"Lawn's done, baby." Finn slid his body between her and the island.

"I can smell that," she said, waving her hand in front of her nose. "You need a shower, mister."

He grabbed onto her hips and pressed kisses down her neck. "Why don't you join me?"

A wet cloth smacked him in the face, and the sound of guys' laughter filled his ears. Sgt. Finley Hunt woke in his bunk with a start, with morning wood and two of his fellow Marines standing around, laughing at him.

"Ooh, baby." Marshall turned his back and wrapped his hands around his neck, making kissing noises as Grant bent over and slapped his knee.

Finn threw the wet washcloth at Marshall's back. "You ruined a perfectly good dream, assholes."

"Better us than the commander. Now let's get going. We got P.T."

"Yeah, yeah. I hear you. I'll hit the shower."

Marshall and Grant left for the mess hall while Finn made up his bunk. Someone had carved "Home Sweet Hellhole" in the wall next to the wooden frame and they weren't wrong. Today was hotter than hell. And he was getting too old for these young guys' shenanigans. Honestly, if it weren't for his sniping skills, he would have accepted a desk job years ago. But he didn't know who he was without his sharpshooting. He didn't have anything else to bring to the table.

After he got back to base on Okinawa, he'd see about a different assignment. He wanted that dream to be a reality. A sweet wife at home, a house, the white picket fence, everything. As the lukewarm shower started up, Finn scrubbed down quickly. He hadn't seen her face in the dream, and now he couldn't even recall her hair color.

Fuck, when was the last time he even got laid? He'd see if Vasquez was up for a round. One of the few female Marines, he'd scratched the itch with her before. It was good, no strings fun. They were far better as friends, so feelings were never going to get involved. They knew they weren't each other's forever. Someday, though, he'd find the one who was.

Seven more years until he was done with the Marines. Once he retired, he could see about getting his own American dream. In the meantime, he better get some breakfast, so he didn't puke running laps.

Josie Anderson curled up on the floor with the other girls, the thin sundress she'd been given not providing much warmth. They were all in similar states of dress and tended to huddle together for warmth. She'd lost track of how many girls and guys had come and gone, lost track of the days since Brad had sold her into slavery as well. It was hard to carve tick marks in a wall when you got moved around every few days. She didn't even have a clue where they were right now.

The boat had brought them to a dock slip last night, and the guys in charge of them had forced them into what could have been a lovely family home on the outside. But the windows on this side of the house were boarded to keep them from waving for help.

She hadn't seen the sun in ages, and she hadn't felt hunger in just as long.

Shaking her head, Josie turned her focus to the other girls in the room. Many of them wore exhaustion like a cloak, but forced themselves to stay alert. Others had already fallen asleep, leaning against a friend.

It had gotten around pretty quickly that she was a nurse. She couldn't legally consider herself one, not really, but considering nothing going on here was legal, she didn't think anyone would block her from getting her license. If she ever got away, that was. The first time she'd tried, they'd beaten her black and blue. But when she tried again, the sneaky asshole that had been watching them had realized punishing her did nothing. But punishing the young girl who'd attached herself to Josie like a little sister did wonders. She hadn't tried to escape since.

They'd been separated at the last stop, and Josie didn't want to think about what had become of the young redhead. And she knew they'd just pick a different girl to punish if she tried to run away again.

Josie was at her wits' end.

"Josie...?" a timid voice said. Then a cough. Kayla crawled forward around the other girls and slumped next to her on the crappy mattress on the floor. "I don't feel so good."

Without a thermometer, Josie had to determine approximate temperatures with the back of her hand. "You're burning up, Kayla. It feels like at least a hundred."

Kayla coughed again, a rattling sound. "I can hardly breathe."

Josie scrubbed a hand over her face. What she wouldn't give for proper diagnostic tools and a *doctor*. Once in a while, when customers complained, the syndicate would allow a girl to go to a clinic wherever they were. She'd be accompanied by one of their colleagues masquerading as a family member, but at least they would get the care they needed.

"Rest for a bit, okay? I'll see if I can get some help." The other girls stared at her.

"Josie, no. I'll be okay."

"You need a doctor."

"They'll hurt you!"

But she had to try.

Rising to her feet, Josie walked across the small bedroom to the door, where she knew a guard stood on the other side. When she tried to open it, it was locked from the outside.

She banged on the hollow wooden obstacle. "Hey! I need to talk to you." When the door opened, she was met with a withering glare.

"What the hell do you want now?"

"Kayla needs to see a doctor. She's deathly sick and running a fever."

"No."

"If she's contagious, we'll all be sick soon. And so will the rest of you."

"I said, no."

How could she work this to her advantage? Josie cringed as she stuck her bare foot in the way when he tried to slam the door shut.

"You mean to tell me that the syndicate won't care if you endanger your precious merchandise? That customers are going to want to have sex with a girl crawling with germs?" She'd heard them called merchandise so many times in the past, however many months she'd been captive, that her stomach barely churned when she used the term herself.

He poked his head into the room, but she didn't think he even knew which one was Kayla. "Looks fine to me."

"I'm telling you, she's running a fever and needs to see a doctor!" Shouting came over his radio, so she raised her voice even louder. "I'm a nurse and I know what I'm talking about!"

"Shut up, bitch!" He backhanded her, and pain erupted in her skull as her head snapped to the side. The girls screamed as her world went black.

ON THE LAPTOP SCREEN, Finn watched as his little sister's boyfriend kneeled in front of her and reached inside a pouch on his hip, pulling out a ring. *Nadia, you have rescued me in so many ways. You rescued my dad from the thief he hired. You helped me heal from my mother's abandonment. You showed me I deserve love and rescued me from a boring life. You're strong, stubborn —"*

"Hear, hear!" cried Roger, and Finn's grin matched his oldest brother's. The outburst drew laughs from the people surrounding the couple.

The camera's angle captured the moment when Nadia stuck her tongue out at him, then turned back to Caleb, who was shaking his head.

"—and I wouldn't change a single thing. Even when we're arguing, you make me want to be a better man. And there's no one else I'd rather fight through life with."

Finn blinked hard at the prickling in his eyes, watching this video for the third or fourth time. He wasn't sure.

"Nadia Lynn Hunt, will you marry me?"

Nadia's tearful voice carried across the world to his headphones. *"Caleb Gray, I am covered in dirt and sweat, my bun is coming undone, and you're asking me... to marry you?"* He bit his lip and nodded, still kneeling in the grass. *"My answer... is YES!"*

She screamed the last word, and the whole clearing applauded and cheered. Caleb wore the biggest grin as he slipped the ring on her finger, stood up, and bent her back in a deep kiss. When he pulled her upright, her four best friends descended on them in a tearful group hug.

The video stopped on the last frame, a tableau of joy and happiness. He'd known it was coming; Caleb had warned them before his deployment that he intended to ask Nadia to marry him. In the email Roger had sent with the attachment, he'd explained how he and Jon had staged a LARP event to set up Caleb's proposal. Finn couldn't be prouder of the men he called brothers, and the one about to be his brother-in-law. Letting Nadia's character rescue Caleb's fit his little sister perfectly.

He only wished he'd been there for it. But his job was half a world away. And there was no small part of him that envied Caleb and Nadia their happiness, while wishing it for them as well.

Someday, he told himself. *Someday that will be me, when I can leave this life behind.* Finn had started protecting his sister from the day she was born when he was six, standing his action figures up around her nursery. Protecting her from afar was a lot less fun, but much more effective.

"Yo, Hunt! You still in here?"

He lifted the headphones off his head to see Marshall and Grant at the door to the computer room. "What is it?"

"You up for some beer pong?"

Finn rolled his eyes. Beer pong at his age should be illegal. But if he said that to the young bucks on his team, they'd just harass him for being old. "Sure, I'll come whoop your asses." He logged out of the computer and set the headphones back on their stand.

"In your dreams."

"Grant, I've been playing beer pong since you were in high school. I think I got this."

Marshall cackled. "This oughta be good."

Chapter 2

JOSIE FLEW OVER A city at night, safe in the arms of her hero. Far away from Brad and the syndicate, their customers that she'd been forced to serve. Nothing could touch her.

As soon as she realized it was merely a dream, her altitude faltered.

Suddenly she was falling, falling, falling...

Josie came back to awareness, pain thumping the side of her head that the thug hadn't hit. She must have whacked her head on something. The hard floor beneath her wasn't doing anything for her comfort, so she rolled to her back, letting out a small groan as she did. Light pierced her eyelids. Shit, were they back for more? What was going on? Why were the other girls so quiet?

Squinting, she raised a hand to shield her eyes from that intense beam of light until it was directed away from her. An unfamiliar voice met her ears.

"It's okay. I'm here to rescue you."

Was she still dreaming? No, the pain was too real for that. Her eyes opened wider to see a woman shining the flashlight on herself. She was dressed in head-to-toe black, face paint obscuring her features, but a few strands of red hair peeked out from beneath her beanie.

"I'm Jenna. Can I help you sit up?" Reaching out a hand, Josie hesitated before grasping it. If this was one of the syndicate's tricks, she'd pay the price either way. But if the offer of help was real, she couldn't risk turning it down. Jenna kneeled and angled the flashlight away.

"I'm Josie." Looking around the room, she realized not only had she made it to the foyer somehow, but they were also alone. "Where is everyone? How did I get here?"

"They uh, they left. Someone was dragging you down the stairs when I broke in. We couldn't catch them."

"We?"

"Come on, let's get you someplace else. There are too many cameras in here for my liking. I'll explain as we go."

Josie had been monitored since the day she was taken. So that didn't surprise her a bit. She ignored the way the room swam.

Jenna's conversation was a helpful distraction from her headache. "So I didn't come alone. There's two guys with me."

"Guys?" Josie hated the tremor in her voice, but she couldn't help it. She'd been at the mercy of too many men lately. Her legs clamped shut in response, a dry ache between them.

Jenna waved her through the house the way she'd been marched just yesterday, to the kitchen in the back. The back door opened onto a walkway to the boat slip, and she wondered if she could make a run for it once she got outside.

"Right, I guess that's not very reassuring." Jenna bit her lip and seemed to think a moment. "Okay, so outside is my boyfriend, Roger, and his friend, Sam. They look like big meanies, but they're good guys."

"O-okay." Even if it turned out to be a lie, it would be easier to run from three people than the whole syndicate.

"You're safe, I promise."

The back door hung open, and Jenna walked through first. Josie followed her on shaky legs, unsure what she was going to find. She tripped and had to cling to Jenna's arm for balance.

"Gentlemen, this is Josie. Josie, this is my boyfriend Roger, and his best friend, Sam."

Josie gripped Jenna's arm tighter. Two tall men dressed in camouflage waved. The slightly leaner one with blonde curls and glasses waved when she said Sam, while Roger had dark brown hair. Both wore dark face paint, giving them a terrifying look.

Sam approached them slowly. "Jenna, she can't walk to the car like that. Her feet..." Jenna looked down, and Josie fidgeted. The night air on her bare legs hadn't fully registered. She hadn't been allowed shoes since the night she was taken. It made running away harder. Not that it'd stopped her trying.

Jenna pursed her lips. "Shit. I don't think we should move the car. The less footage Frankie has to delete, the better."

Before Josie could ask who Frankie was, Roger put a finger to his ear. "Hey Frankie, change the codes on the doors, okay? We want the FBI to get as much evidence as possible." He nodded. Whoever Frankie was, they were obviously not there on the ground.

Shivers racked her frame, though she tried to hide it. The threadbare sundress didn't offer much protection from the chill. Sam's gentle voice caught her attention. "Josie, how about I carry you over to our car and we get out of here?"

Jenna kept talking. "You're welcome to stay with us if you want, or we can try to get you home."

Josie shook her head. "I don't even know where I am. They didn't tell us where they were taking us."

"You're in Baltimore, Maryland." Jenna told her, and Josie went numb. Her vision blurred as she brought her hands to her mouth.

"It's so far…" she sobbed.

Jenna wrapped an arm around her. "Let's get you somewhere safe for now. We can figure out the details later."

Sam turned his back and crouched. At first, Josie didn't understand what he was trying to do. But Jenna helped Josie get on his back, piggyback style. It was awkward, but efficient, and there was no groping like there certainly would have been with her captors. She wrapped her arms around Sam's shoulders, and he took off, the four of them weaving through the tall grass to the woods. Roger pulled a tarp off a strangely shaped lump, revealing an SUV. He stuffed the tarp into the trunk, where he proceeded to secure his weapons. Josie hadn't even realized he'd had a gun, but of course he'd need it to raid the syndicate's house.

Sam dipped down to set Josie in the backseat, and when he turned around he gasped. He reached out to probe her head where it ached, and she flinched. Sam yanked his hand back with a grimace.

"We should take you to the hospital."

Her lower lip trembled. "One of them hit me in the head and I passed out. When I woke up, Jenna was there. And everyone else was gone."

Sam looked at Roger. "She could have a concussion. We need a professional."

Roger looked down at himself. "We can't go in there looking like this."

Jenna pulled makeup wipes out of her bag in the back. "Here, boys. This will help. We should stop at home and find her some shoes. And a sweater."

Sam jolted a bit, like something startled him. When he turned his head, she spied an earpiece nestled into his ear, where a faint noise that sounded like someone speaking came from.

"We'll ask. See you at home, Frankie." Jenna took her earpiece out and clicked it off, and Roger followed suit. Sam shut her door then waited a moment, speaking privately to whoever was on the line, before climbing into the SUV's passenger side. Jenna pulled herself into the backseat with Josie.

"We're going to stop at Roger's house so we can all change clothes and wash our faces," Jenna explained. "My friend Frankie is there. She's going to find some more clothes for you."

"T-thank you," Josie stammered.

"Hey, babe, turn the heat up back here? She's still shivering."

"You got it." Warm air began to blow on Josie, making the raised goose bumps on her skin relax.

Josie was silent, watching the darkened world go by. It'd had been so long since she had seen the sky. But the moon shone down in a sliver of light, stars twinkling through the trees. The only lights on the road were theirs.

Actually, now that she thought about it, how long had it been?

"What day is it?"

Silence filled the car. "November fourteenth," Jenna replied gently.

Josie took a shaky breath and then another. Six months. Six long months of captivity.

But she'd survived it.

And now she was in an unfamiliar place, with unfamiliar people. But something, her gut feelings, told her she could trust them.

Not that her instincts had been all that great with Brad.

No, that wasn't fair. She'd been caught up in the fairy tale that he spun, so distracted that she ignored the voice in her head that had told her not to go with him. Still, Josie made herself a vow. No more men. She would stand on her own two feet before she got into another relationship. If she ever wanted one, that is.

She closed her eyes and prayed to a God she wasn't sure she believed in that these new friends proved trustworthy.

FINN WIPED THE SWEAT from his brow and fixed his helmet back on his head.

"I should have brought some dough from the kitchen. We coulda had cookies baking in the Humvee while we were on patrol."

He grinned at Vasquez, her short dark ponytail glistening in the sun. "Don't think the cooks would appreciate that."

She shrugged. "Depends on whether we brought them back any. I can't imagine it's pleasant cooking all day in this heat."

"At least the base has air conditioning." Hartmann cracked his neck, motioning them back into the vehicle. "Let's get going."

Finn followed his unit leader's order, buckling himself into the back seat. Nicholson took the other side. Hartmann sat behind the wheel and Grant sat next to him. Grant, Finn, and Vasquez kept their weapons in hand in case someone shot at them.

He caught Vasquez's eye and waggled his eyebrows. Gesturing "you and me?" with his hand was his usual way of asking if she wanted to blow off some steam. She winked back at him with a grin and a nod. That was their code. It meant she'd meet him at their usual rendezvous once they'd filled out their reports. Simple and effective.

Fraternizing wasn't exactly frowned upon, as long as neither Marine reported to the other and they weren't married to someone else. But that's not what this was between them. They were friends who fucked, nothing more. He'd decided not to get involved when he enlisted. Sex was just an itch to be scratched.

They were rolling along the desert road; the heat making the scenery wavy. They didn't get more than halfway back to base, though.

Out of nowhere, a fireball erupted in front of him, the ear-shattering explosion rocketing the Humvee up into the air as they shouted. It started to flip in the air, but came down on its side in a cloud of dust.

Fire. Heat. Searing pain. Screams. And then, nothing.

Chapter 3

FEELING MUCH WARMER WITH the leggings and hoodie Jenna had loaned her, Josie trailed behind the redhead into the emergency room. Her eyes darted around, noting the security guards and the other waiting patients. No one looked threatening, and she breathed a sigh of relief. It didn't make sense for these nice people to rescue her and then take her right back. But the anxiety of living on the edge for half a year wouldn't go away overnight.

"Good evening. How can I help you?"

"My friend got hit in the head, and we're concerned it might be a concussion."

"Okay, can you give me your name and date of birth?"

Josie gripped the edge of the triage desk, carefully angling her head so the nurse could see the blood Sam had found in her hair. "Josephine Anderson." She rattled off her birthdate, but when he asked for address and identification, she looked at Jenna in fear.

Jenna rattled off an address, and the guy looked between them. "Don't you remember where you live, hun?"

"I, uh, I…"

Jenna leaned over and whispered. "Can we discuss this in private? It's a sensitive subject."

"Sure. Come on back." He gestured them over to a small office. "We use it when we're really busy for additional triage." Once the door was shut, Jenna looked at her.

"Um, I was just rescued from … traffickers." Josie hated the way her voice trembled. "They hit me and I blacked out, so my … new friends wanted to get it checked out."

His entire demeanor changed on a dime. "How long were you with them?"

"I'm not sure… it was May when I was…" Oh God. Tears. Why was she crying *now*?

"Okay honey, you want me to call the police?"

"We're already working with the FBI." Jenna stiffened. Josie wasn't sure why. Maybe the FBI didn't want local police stepping on their toes.

"I'll have to run it by my manager, but if you already have a contact... I think I can say it's already handled."

"We do. I can give you his name and number if you want."

"That won't be necessary. But keep a hold of your records from this visit today, in case they need them for the report, okay?"

Josie nodded and winced. Now that she wasn't so cold, the pain was becoming more apparent.

"Okay, why don't the two of you hang right here, and I'll go see about getting you a bed."

"Thank you." Jenna smiled and sat in the chair next to Josie as the nurse shut the door. "Getting warmer?"

"Y-yeah. A little." Pretty sure shock was setting in now, Josie pulled her hands inside her sleeves and tucked one into the other. Jenna had her arm wrapped loosely around her.

It didn't take as long as Josie would have expected for the nurse to return with a wheelchair. "Here you go. We're going to take you and your friend back to your room and then the doctor will be in, okay?"

Josie sat in the wheelchair and propped her feet up on the supports. The nurse wheeled them back into a maze of hallways. This was clearly a big hospital, though the beds were mostly empty for now. She knew that could change at a moment's notice, though.

He wheeled her into a room and Jenna followed behind. She rose out of the chair and sat on the bed.

"I'm going to get your vitals. Someone will be in to talk with you soon, okay?" Josie nodded. The routine of getting her temperature, pulse ox, and blood pressure relaxed her.

"Hmm, blood pressure's a bit low. How much water have you drunk today?"

Josie shook her head. "I had a bit at the house when we stopped, but other than that, not much."

He clucked his tongue. "I'm pretty sure they're going to put you on fluids, and it's standard procedure to fit you with an IV, anyway. So I'll call your nurse and see about getting that started. Have a good night, Josie. I hope your head feels better."

"Thanks." She lay back on the bed, a more comfortable mattress than she'd seen in months.

Jenna sat in the folding chair next to her bed. "I'll text Roger, let him know we got a room."

She typed away on her phone. "Huh. Apparently, you only get one support person back here with you." She shrugged and put her phone down. "I told him to watch some television and get some coffee. We're probably going to be awhile."

"I'm sorry about this."

Josie grabbed her hand. "You don't have anything to be sorry for, Josie. This is not your fault. I would rather stay so you feel safe, okay?"

"Okay."

"Hunt, do you copy?"

"I got a pulse."

"Tourniquet, now!"

Finn's head swam in the darkness. Voices drifted across the void from far away. He heard the whir of a fan, but couldn't feel the breeze on his face.

"Chopper's here."

"Alright, let's move!"

"Go, go, go!"

Machines beeped, calls for the nurses ringing out through the ward. The transport team wheeled Josie right past them into Radiology.

"Here, let's get you into the CT machine."

She got up from her bed and laid down on the board. Two foam blocks were placed on either side of her head. "Keep very still. We only want to do this once."

Josie closed her eyes. While she wouldn't sleep until they got the all-clear from the doctor, it felt nice to pretend for the moment it took to scan her head. Afterward she was ushered back onto the gurney and wheeled back through the double doors into the emergency department. Hopefully they'd get the results soon.

"He's crashing!"

"Don't you die on me, motherfucker!"

"Clear!"

Finn fell into blissful unconsciousness.

"The front desk said you don't have any identification on you?"

"That's correct." The doctor facing her seemed indifferent, but Josie figured she was just trying to do her job. At one point Josie had thought she might end up working in the ED and she could understand needing to distance yourself emotionally from the job.

"Can you tell me what happened?"

So Josie did. How six months ago, her boyfriend sold her into human trafficking. How she'd been used and abused, and how she didn't have any of her identification with her because it had been left in Montana with the rat. How she'd tried to advocate for the girls to get care when they were sick, and how the syndicate thug backhanded her for talking back.

"My head went this way, and then I blacked out. When I came to, they were all gone, and Jenna was there to get me out."

The doctor cut a look over at Jenna. "You know the patient?"

"We only just met. But when my colleague from the FBI saw the blood in her hair, he felt it best we get her checked out immediately." The doctor nodded. While they waited, Jenna had explained to Josie that Sam worked for the FBI and while he couldn't actually help with this case since it wasn't his department, he knew someone who could. She'd have to tell the story again to the agent, which she dreaded. The more she talked about it, the more real everything felt.

"Well, Miss Anderson, you have a mild concussion and your neck is sprained. Based on your BMI, you're also malnourished, so I want you to drink lots of fluids and increase your food intake *slowly*." She emphasized the word. "You don't want to overwhelm your system. Small meals, even if you're not hungry. Go for things rich in nutrients and calories. A multivitamin wouldn't be a bad idea, either. I also recommend finding a PCP and following up with them." Then she paused and adjusted her glasses. "After the ordeal you've been through, I'd also recommend you talk to someone. I can give you a list of therapists specializing in these situations, if you'd like them."

Josie was already feeling more lively with the fluids running through her, but she knew from her studies this wouldn't be an overnight solution. "Yes, please."

The doctor checked something off on her tablet and then headed for the door. "I've sent the discharge orders. Once that bag of fluids is done, you're free to go. Take care, Miss Anderson."

"Thank you!" She looked over at Jenna. She leaned back in the folding chair, looking like she was going to take a nap against the wall. "Are you sure it's okay for me to stay with you?"

"Of course!" Jenna sat up like she'd been electrocuted. "I wouldn't pull you out of that hellhole just to abandon you!"

"But you don't ... you don't even know me." Josie couldn't help the insecurity. It seemed with her rehydration, her brain was coming back online and overthinking things. "Why would you come after me in the first place?"

"Well, we were coming after anyone that was being held there." Jenna bit her lip. "We wanted to rescue more of you, but it didn't go very well."

"I'm sorry." She hated that the only reason she was here was because she'd been unconscious.

"You have nothing to apologize for."

Josie shook her head. "No, I mean, I want them out of there, too. Those girls are so young, and they ... shouldn't be exposed to that... that..."

"There really isn't a word that's awful enough to describe those people, is there?" Jenna murmured. She reached out and placed her hand over Josie's. "Well, this was officially more of an evidence-finding mission to convince the big guns to come help us. And what's better than an eyewitness account?"

Josie nodded. She'd do whatever the FBI asked her to do to get those girls and guys out of the syndicate's clutches. She swore it to them, then and there. She wouldn't abandon them.

With that, the alarm on her IV machine went off. The nurse bustled in. "I have your discharge papers here." She handed them to Josie as she turned off the alarm. "Let me just get this flushed and then you'll be out of here!"

Five minutes later, Josie was dressed in her strange outfit and the two of them walked down the hallway back to the waiting room. Poor Roger looked beat, dark circles under his eyes, and several paper coffee cups were on the table next to him. He stared at a television screen on the wall so intently that he didn't notice they were there until Jenna poked him in the arm.

"We're done."

He shook his head and ran his gaze over Josie, but not in the leering way she was used to. He was just assessing her. "Your color looks much better."

"They gave me IV fluids for dehydration."

"She's also got a concussion, and a sprained neck. And the doctor wants her to find a PCP."

"So take it easy, hmm?" Roger nodded, agreeing with himself.

"What's wrong, babe? You're staring at CNN like it insulted your mother." Jenna cocked her head at her boyfriend.

"See that ticker at the bottom?" He pointed. "A roadside bomb hit an American convoy. They're reporting two deaths but aren't releasing what unit got hit. It just happened today."

Jenna's voice softened. "You're worried about Finn?"

He nodded. "I'll call Jon when we get home."

"Will he know anything?"

Roger shrugged. "He might. He's got the right clearances for it."

Jenna must have noticed her confusion, because she hooked her arm through Josie's while they headed for the parking garage. "Roger is the oldest of four. There's three boys, and a girl. Nadia is the youngest, then Finn, and Jon is the second oldest. Finn and Jon are still in the military, but Finn is the one who's deployed right now. He's a Marine."

"But they didn't say if it was a Marine unit?"

"No. So it might not be him at all." Roger ran a hand through his hair. "I think I had too much coffee. Let's go get doughnuts and take them back to the house for everyone. I need something sweet."

Josie's mouth watered. "I haven't had a doughnut in *ages*."

Jenna gave her a grin. "Sounds like just what the doctor ordered."

Chapter 4

FINN SQUINTED AGAINST THE sunlight piercing the blinds of his hospital room. Not for the first time, he considered calling the nurse in to close them, since he couldn't very well get up and do it himself. He didn't know what day it was, or how long he'd been here, wherever *here* was. The brightness stabbing his head with pain was the only reason he knew it was daytime; last time he'd woken up here, it had been nighttime.

He dreamed so often and so vividly that he wasn't entirely certain what was real. Was this a dream? It seemed a fitting respite from the explosions and fighting. Normally he could turn off his emotions to get through a battle, but anymore he found himself shouting and opening his eyes in this very hospital room, covered in sweat and howling in pain. Up was down, left had gone right, and time meant nothing anymore. Only to close his eyes and end up back in the fray once again.

The next time he awoke and saw the plain beige walls and heard the quiet beep of various machines, a nurse stood next to him. "How are you feeling?"

His right arm was on fire. "Hurts," he grunted. He couldn't move it, or his right leg, at all. His eyes strained to read the whiteboard across the room, but the words were blurry. He'd always had perfect vision. Hell, his nickname had been Eagle Eye since high school. It had to be the pain.

The nurse nodded and adjusted a dial. "That should help."

Almost immediately, the pain eased up. Finn fought the familiar drowsiness coming over him again. He had to at least get a drink before going back to the desert. "Water?"

"Sure." She held a cup with a straw out to him, and he had never tasted anything sweeter.

He thought he heard her say something about surgery in the morning as he relaxed back against the pillows. Finn had a score to settle with some insurgents.

HE HEARD THE SOUNDS of the hospital once more, and he panted in relief, dimly aware of being soaked in his own sweat yet again. Finn's eyelids weighed a ton, but he heard someone speaking, so he wrenched them open with a groan.

"He's awake!"

"Ma'am, you can't see him yet."

"But..."

"Come on, Judy. Let the man do his job."

"I promise we'll come get you as soon as he's cleared for visitors."

That sounded like his parents. But he was in the Middle East. How?

"Sergeant Hunt?"

His throat hurt like hell and he was thirstier than a teenage girl at a boy band concert. Squinting his eyes, he saw someone in a white lab coat standing next to a man in a uniform he knew all too well. "Lieutenant... Stevenson?"

His commanding officer spoke in an unusually kind tone. "Are you back with us, Finn?"

Taking stock of his surroundings, he found himself in a hospital bed, bandages wrapped around his right leg. His right arm throbbed with a dull ache, but he attempted a salute, anyway. And he could see okay if he closed the right eye. "Yes, sir."

"At ease, son."

He may have been drowsy, but the tone of the CO's voice told Finn something was very wrong. The CO pulled up a chair and sat down next to Finn's head, which eased the strain on his eyes. "Do you know where you are?"

"No, sir."

Stevenson looked him straight in the eye and blew Finn's life apart. "Hunt, you're at the hospital at the base in Germany. We had to evac you out of the combat zone."

Finn had been so out of it. He wasn't even sure how long it had been since he was last with his unit. "What... what happened?"

"The patrol truck hit a roadside bomb. You and Vasquez were the only survivors." The lieutenant's mouth pressed into a grim line. "And it's not looking good for her."

Flashes of his dreams came back to Finn. But no, this wasn't real. Was it?

"If I may, sir." The man in the white coat interrupted his CO, who stood and let the doctor sit down in his place. "Hi, Finn. I'm Doctor Barnett. You sustained serious injuries in the back seat of that truck. We removed as much shrapnel as we could from your leg, but I'm afraid we couldn't get all of it. I believe based on that squint, that your right eye also suffered damage, so we'll need to get you an eye exam once you're more healed. Later we can discuss your prosthesis options."

Confusion wrinkled Finn's brow as the fog of whatever drugs he'd been on lifted. "Prosthesis? What for?"

The two men looked nervously at each other and then back at Finn. Regret shone in his commanding officer's eyes. "I'm so sorry, son. The blast took your ..."

Seeing Stevenson speechless and merely nodding at the other side of the bed, something completely out of character, caused Finn to look in the same direction.

The blood ran out of his face, and he shook with chills. Alarms started going off, and the doctor yelled at someone in the hall to bring blankets, and something else about blood pressure dropping. But Finn was frozen in that hospital bed.

Because when he looked at his right arm, his dominant side, his trigger hand... there was nothing but a stump wrapped in bandages where his elbow had once been.

NADIA PULLED UP TO the house in an old brown Chevy sedan and honked the horn. Jenna grabbed the basket of cleaning supplies as Josie opened the door.

"Good luck with the apartment, Frankie and Sam!" Jenna called up the stairs.

"See you later!" came the answer. Frankie had turned out to be a sweetheart, a Black woman who sassed Sam to no end. And he loved it.

Their dynamic had been fun to watch, as had the one between Jenna and Roger. Josie only hoped once she got on her feet, if she decided to get into another relationship, that she could be as strong as these women.

"Hey, let me help carry that." Nadia took the basket from Jenna. Her long reddish-brown hair that matched Roger's had been pulled up in a ponytail. "I appreciate your help so much, you guys."

"It's not like I have much going on," Josie said with a hesitant smile. Yes, she was waiting for Ross, Sam's FBI contact, to get in touch regarding the investigation, and she was supposed to lie low until it was over. But she'd been going nuts not having anything to do and had taken to cleaning Roger's house from top to bottom since he wouldn't hear of her paying rent. It was so clean she didn't have anything else left, so when Nadia asked Jenna if she'd help clean her parents' house, Josie had jumped at the chance to assist.

"Oh, please thank your friend for the clothes. They fit perfectly." The two of them trailed Nadia to her car, where she popped the trunk and set the cleaning supplies inside.

"Great! Jade will be thrilled someone could get some use out of them."

"Shotgun!" cried Jenna, and they piled into the car.

Nadia laughed as she turned the key. "Jon's taking care of the lawn today, so we might have a smelly guy hanging around."

"Well, he better not get the house messy after we're done." Jenna clicked her seat belt, and Josie followed suit.

"He likes his balls too much to do something that fucking dumb." Nadia turned her car around and headed back down the gravel driveway to the main road.

The language had been one of the first things she'd noticed about this group. Where Josie grew up, swearing was forbidden, and she usually didn't even *think* a curse word unless the situation was severe. Brad? The syndicate? She'd cuss them out all day long. But she wasn't in her parents' little community anymore, and she had no intention of going back. And the rest of the world cussed. Liberally.

She'd get used to it, eventually.

"When will your parents get home?" she asked as they drove.

"I'm not sure. Mom said they're waiting for the doctor to give them a time frame. They got to see him yesterday, and she was …" Nadia's voice faltered. Jenna reached over the console and squeezed her shoulder.

"Did she say how bad it was?" Jenna asked gently.

The words were clearly difficult for her. "He… he lost his right arm."

Both Josie and Jenna sucked air through their teeth at that.

But when Nadia pulled up to her parents' driveway next to a large red pickup truck, she shook herself out of her sadness. "Well, at least I can make sure the house is clean for when they get home."

"And we're here to help." Jenna reminded her.

As they unloaded the car and made trips to the front porch, a tall, clean cut, and muscular man Josie vaguely remembered from the engagement party came around the front. "Hey, baby sister."

Nadia rolled her eyes. "Hello, old man."

"I am not!"

She gave him a wicked grin. "If I'm your baby sister, that makes you an old man."

"You're twelve years younger than me. You're *always* going to be my baby sister."

Nadia narrowed her eyes. "Josie, this is my older brother, Jonathon. He's a terrible flirt, so don't mind him."

"I am not. I'm very good at flirting." He reached out a hand, and Josie stared at it, wondering if she should shake it. Before things got too awkward, she decided she'd better.

"Nice to meet you again."

But instead of shaking it, he bowed over her hand and kissed the back of it. "The pleasure's all mine."

Josie jumped and pulled her hand back, tucking herself behind Jenna.

"Down, boy." Jenna growled. His playfulness evaporated as Jon blinked at her, then raised his hands and took two steps back.

"Not sure what I did, but I'm sorry. I meant no offense."

Nadia's gaze flicked between Jenna and Jon. She held out the bucket of cleaning supplies she'd brought. "You wanna help us clean?"

"I just finished the lawn, Nad. I'm wiped, and I need a shower."

"Are you coming for Thanksgiving?"

He scoffed. "Where else would I be?"

"Good. You and Roger get to figure out how to roast the bird."

He looked confused for a second, then smacked his forehead. "Oh right. We still don't know when Mom and Dad will be home."

Nadia nodded. "Mom said we should still have dinner here, since they have the most room. She just wants us to clean up after."

"And you're cleaning now?"

Nadia huffed. "I'm off work for the week and I need to do *some*thing."

Jon held out his arms, and she went in for a hug. Jenna nudged Josie. "We'll go in and start working on a game plan, Nadia.""Okay."

Josie followed Jenna inside. She guessed sometimes a girl just needed her big brother to tell her everything was going to be okay. *That must be a nice thing to have,* she thought to herself.

"Are you okay?" Jenna asked her as soon as they were inside. "I forgot to warn you about him. He acts like a sleazy playboy, but Mama Hunt wouldn't put up with it in reality."

Shame came down on her like a too-tight coat. "I didn't mean to overreact."

"No no no, that's not what I meant." Jenna shook her head furiously. "Listen, he has to learn to tone it down. Or at least learn when it's appropriate. He's a grown-ass man." Jenna set the bucket of cleaning supplies on the rustic wooden coffee table in the living room.

"Ew, you stink! Go shower," Nadia shouted as she opened the front door and shut it behind her. "Why are boys so gross?"

Daily showers felt like an incredible luxury after her time in captivity. The faces of the girls she'd known flitted through her mind. She sent up a prayer to the God she wasn't sure really existed again, that Agent Patterson would find them and set them free.

The door banged open, and Jon attacked Nadia with another hug. "Ew! No!" she shrieked in anger. Her scream seemed to trip a wire in Josie's brain.

Screams echoed from behind the locked door where Kadie had been taken. "I like it when they scream and put up a fight," one customer said to another as they waited for their turn.

"Josie? Josie!" Jenna's hand gripped her shoulder, pulling her back to Earth. "Are you okay?"

She looked up from where she'd curled behind the armchair. How did she get back there?

"I, uh, I'm okay. Fine." She accepted Jenna's hand to help her stand and ran a hand over her hair that she'd pulled back.

"Jon's gone," Nadia said with concern on her face. "I'm sorry I yelled."

"It's f-fine, Nadia." Josie released a shaky breath and straightened her shoulders. "Where do you want to start?"

Chapter 5

Violet peered around the corner, her ears perked for the boss's footsteps. Her journalist senses were tingling, that she was almost to the juicy bits of information. Creeping down the hallway, she rubbed at the fake beard she'd started wearing when she took this assignment.

Her alter ego, Victor, was a new recruit for Nautical Transit, and she was determined to get to the bottom of how a floundering business was still in operation.

Part of the problem is the misogyny, she thought to herself. They wouldn't accept her for a warehouse position as a female, so she'd had to fake a male identity just to get the interview.

"What do you *mean,* you lost one?" Norman's voice didn't sound happy. "How hard is it to move a shipment of merchandise?"

She couldn't hear what the flunky on the other side of the line was saying. But by the huffing and puffing coming from her boss's office, it wasn't acceptable.

"Put him on the phone." He waited a beat. "How many times do I have to tell you not to damage the merchandise?"

Violet crept closer. She'd been summoned at the end of her shift, but her mama always taught her not to interrupt when someone was on the phone. And she'd discovered as a teen that was the best time to eavesdrop.

"Oh, this one had a mouth on her, did she? It's your fault you lost her. Now find her before she runs her mouth again. We already know the cameras were tapped. You're only lucky the FBI didn't find anything when they went through the safehouse. And bring her alive. I want to question her myself."

Violet's heart pounded in her chest so loud she was sure it could be heard in the dimly lit hallway. Women? The merchandise was *women?*

Thoughts warred in her head. Leaving this early would mean she didn't have enough for her article, but if she got in any deeper, they'd never let her alter ego go.

Evidence. She needed evidence. And she had to call her editor tonight. This was way bigger than either of them had anticipated.

Her mind made up, she waited until the phone slammed down into its cradle. Then she turned the corner.

"Hey, boss. You wanted to see me?" Thank goodness for her natural contralto range. She sounded just like a young man in his twenties, which was who she'd told them she was.

"Victor! Jesus, you scared me. Don't sneak up on me like that." His dark, beady eyes examined her for a moment. "Did you hear any of that?"

She shrugged. "Just sounded like someone at the warehouse fucked up."

"You could say that." He pushed back his chair and walked to where she stood in the doorway. "We're about to get a very important shipment, and I need someone to help guard it. Are you interested in the extra hours?"

"Of course." Could this be her big break?

"Now, this is our most important line of business, so you won't be able to talk to anyone about it. It's top secret."

"Yes, sir."

"Alright, I'll add you to the schedule. See you tomorrow."

"See you tomorrow, Norm." She locked her face into calm determination as she strode away, but inside she was giddy. "Victor" had finally earned his place and she would get to see behind the curtain.

And then Violet was going to blow it wide open for all to see.

FINN IGNORED THE HOLLOW feeling in his chest while he went through the motions of his exercises. Physical therapy was not therapeutic, at least not that he'd found so far. But his right leg supported him now, the wounds mostly healed. He'd set off metal detectors for life, most likely, and the pitted skin would probably scar. His eyesight had come back, although his eyes could still be sensitive to bright light. Based on the exam results, he no longer had perfect vision, but he didn't need glasses just yet. Down the road, maybe.

Vasquez hadn't made it. She'd never woken up. He was the lone survivor.

Late at night, when he couldn't sleep, he asked why. Why had they hit the bomb? Why had it fallen on her side? Why was he the only one left? What good was a sniper with one arm?

They hadn't fit his prosthesis yet. Apparently that had to wait until he was back in the States.

"Sergeant Hunt, you're not wearing the stump shrinker again." Doctor Barnett walked into the physical therapy room as he often did during Finn's appointments. "We need to get your swelling down."

Finn hung his head, still walking on the treadmill. "I don't want it to get scrawny." Now that they weren't knocking him out with IV pain killers, he had done some searching on his phone, which the CO had brought from the sandpit with him. Finn had left it behind while he was on patrol that day, so it was safe. He'd seen other patients with... what was it again? Transradial amputations. Finn had worked hard for those biceps ladies loved hanging onto, and he didn't want to lose that, too. He'd be lop-sided!

"You have to bring the swelling down so that it will fit the prosthesis and give you better control. It's not going to erase your muscle mass."

"But I can't do push-ups with the fake arm, right?"

"It depends on what they outfit you with at Walter Reed. You can talk to the doctors there and ask about it. I'm sure they'll have recommendations and guidance should you want to continue your exercise regimen." As he spoke, Doctor Barnett walked over to where Finn had ditched the shrinker when the nurse wasn't looking and paused his treadmill. "But they can only do that if the healing is complete."

Finn sighed, but he let the older man roll the compression sock back onto what once was his elbow.

"If you keep wearing the stump shrinker, and promise to wear it at all times, I can get you discharged and on a plane next week."

Finn started to perk up, but sighed. "I guess."

"I know this is a difficult transition. Do you want to talk to someone?"

Finn shook his head. No, he wasn't ready to see a shrink yet. They'd make him see someone at the VA as soon as he got home, but he was still processing that his unit was gone. That a coward with a bomb had taken them out.

Doctor Barnett sighed, and while Finn had his back to him, he could see the older man run his hand through his white hair in his mind's eye. He'd done it a lot in their appointments. "I don't want to keep you here over the holidays. I can't get you home for Thanksgiving, but I'm sure your family would want to see you for Christmas."

That did it. Mom would freak if he couldn't get home for her favorite holiday. "Okay, Doc. I'll keep it on." Even though it itched something fierce.

Barnett clapped a hand on his shoulder. "Good lad. I'll see you tomorrow." He watched him leave and started the treadmill up again. The doctor was right. His family wanted him for the holidays, so he would go. Not like he had anywhere else to go. They were giving him an honorable discharge and packing up his room at the base in Okinawa as he lay there in the hospital. *Semper Fi*, his ass.

Mom and Dad had been by yesterday on their way to the airport. Her tearful hug hadn't comforted him like it should have. It had been right after he found out about Vasquez. All Mom cared about was her baby boy had survived.

Meanwhile, he couldn't hardly wipe his own ass because he had to learn to use his non-dominant hand for everything. And the pain pills made him feel like his head was floating, so he'd been refusing them as much as he could.

This whole thing sucked donkey balls, and he almost wished it had been him on the other side of their ride.

But, no, he wouldn't do that to his family.

Exhausted after his workout, he laid on the massage table and let the therapist put him through his stretches. When he got back to his room, he'd shower and take another nap.

Thanksgiving morning, Josie, Roger, and Jenna met Nadia and Caleb at the parents' house at nine. Beautiful red and orange leaves littered the lawn, and they crunched under their feet as they walked up to the front door.

"Happy Thanksgiving!" Nadia said as she hugged them each in turn, even Josie. That made her smile. Turned out cleaning together brought people closer. Brad hadn't allowed her to spend time with friends outside of classes, so this was new to her.

Nadia's fiancé resembled a golden retriever faced with a tennis ball. "Hey, Roger, can you help me set up the turkey fryer?"

"Yeah, sure. But Dad always brines it at least a day in advance. It won't be ready."

"No worries." Caleb grinned as he shucked his leather coat and hung it in the coat closet. "I came over and did it."

Josie didn't miss Nadia's eye roll. "Please, *please*, big brother, will you supervise my idiot fiancé as he fries his first turkey? I would like him to make it to the wedding with all his fingers."

Roger chuckled. "Sure, little sister."Jenna raised an eyebrow. "You lost the argument?"

Nadia sighed. "George got all excited for fried turkey and I couldn't break the old man's heart like that."

Jenna chuckled. "Girl, he played you."

Roger cracked his knuckles. "How big a bird did you get?"

Nadia shook her head. "I didn't. Mom had an eighteen-pounder sitting in the freezer."

"Ah," Roger said. "What time are we serving dinner?"

"I'm hoping for three. Then if it's late, it's not a big deal."

"Do you guys usually have such an early dinner?" Josie bit her lip. She wore one of the few dresses she had been gifted for her first holiday meal, a soft brown sweater dress, but she was the only one. Was it overkill? She had no frame of reference except the women with her.

"Mom likes to do the big holiday meals early, so she's not too tired for the cleanup." Nadia led them into the kitchen and proceeded to pull out what appeared to be a graph with times and food listed.

"A spreadsheet, Nad? Really?" Roger crossed his arms.

"Everything has different cooking times, so unless you want something to be cold, I thought it would be for the best." She looked over her plan of attack, and Josie had to admire her organization.

Josie stepped forward. "How can we help?"

"How about we set the table first? Once we're done with that, we have to wash and peel the potatoes." She turned to Roger and Caleb. "You guys go ahead and get the fryer set up, but the turkey can't go in until one-thirty."

Roger saluted, and she smacked her brother on the arm. He and Caleb left through the back door.

"Where are they going?" Jenna asked.

"Dad keeps the turkey fryer in the shed, since we only use it once a year." Nadia explained, leading them to the dining room.

The old-fashioned gold and cream stripe wallpaper highlighted a beautiful mahogany dining set that the girls had just polished on Monday. Nadia pulled a drawer open in the china cabinet and drew out a white tablecloth.

"Here, Josie, take one end." Together, they spread the damask over the table and evened it out. At Nadia's urging, Jenna pulled out beautiful bone china plates edged in gold. Meanwhile, Nadia backtracked to the kitchen to get silverware.

"What does your family usually do for Thanksgiving, Josie?"

Josie looked down at Jenna's expectant face. "They... they don't celebrate it."

Her blue eyes about popped out of her head. "Seriously?"

Josie straightened a fork while her cheeks heated. "They don't believe in holidays. So this is my first time celebrating."

Brad hadn't bothered with holidays, not out of a religious belief, but sheer laziness.

Nadia cleared her throat. "Great. Nothing like pressure, right?"

Josie giggled to set her at ease. "Please don't worry about it. Honestly, you could set a TV dinner in front of me and tell me that was the tradition, and I wouldn't know the difference."

"TV! That reminds me! Did you ever see the parade?"

"Parade?"

Nadia shot out of the dining room in excitement. "Come on!"

Jenna laughed. "I loved watching the Thanksgiving Day parade in New York when I was a kid."

"I thought you grew up in New Mexico."

"I did. But they televise it every year." Jenna led her back into the family room where Nadia had turned on the television.

"Just give it a chance. You have to watch it at least once in your life."

Josie sat down with the girls, her eyes transfixed by the enthusiastic band marching across the screen. Balloons like she'd never seen before floated down the street.

She'd had no idea this went on. And according to the announcers, it had been going on for nearly a hundred years!

During the commercial break, they finished setting the table with the gold china and the sparkling crystal goblets, and cloth napkins. But when she tried to help Nadia and Jenna wash potatoes, they shooed her back to the couch.

"You've been deprived, and we're fixing that. We can handle washing a few pounds of potatoes."

Jenna agreed with Nadia. "Jon's coming to help peel, right?"

"Right. So go. Enjoy."

Josie figured it would be best not to argue with her hostess. "If you need me, call me, okay?"

"We won't." Nadia grinned. Josie chuckled and shook her head.

The last float to come down the parade route was none other than Santa Claus. Of course, a department store hosted the parade, and they wanted to remind people to shop for Christmas gifts.

Josie knew about Santa. It was impossible to exist without knowing about what her parents had called "the pagan side" of Christmas. Not that they celebrated the religious side, since they didn't do holidays. As a child, she'd been jealous of the kids who talked about what they were asking Santa for that year, because she wasn't allowed. She didn't dare voice her envy to her parents, though. Her little brother did once, and Jeb tended to be mouthy, so he'd gotten the belt.

She missed her little brothers and sisters, but not her parents. Who knew what her parents would have told them about their sister's disappearance? She'd come to terms with never seeing them again long ago.

The one time she'd rebelled and stood up for herself, and look how that turned out.

Josie shook off her maudlin thoughts as the front door banged shut. "Lieutenant Hunt reporting for potato duty!"

She spun around to see Jon hanging up a jacket in the coat closet. "Good morning, Josie. Nice to see you again."

"Good morning," she replied, watching him warily. But he didn't make a move to approach her. Merely offered her a nod and headed back for the kitchen.

He wasn't a bad guy. Josie hated how skittish she'd become. She had to do better. And she was going to start by helping in the kitchen.

Her thoughts strayed to the people still in captivity. While her appetite had started to come back, she wished she could share all this bounty with them. Guilt for her good fortune often plagued her, especially at night.

She hoped her new therapist could help with the nightmares.

Chapter 6

"You mean to tell me we had instant mashed potatoes this whole time?"

"It's a holiday, Jon. And it didn't take us *that* long."

Jon held his hands up, holding his hands like his fingers had curled up with arthritis. "I peeled fewer potatoes on the submarine!"

Nadia whacked him on the arm and tutted at him. "Poor baby. You did not. It was only five pounds."

"But the instant would have been so much easier!"

Jenna set her hands on her hips and took up the argument while Nadia dumped the green beans and cream of mushroom soup into a casserole dish. "It's Josie's first ever holiday and you want us to serve instant mashed potatoes? Have you no pride?"

Josie felt her face turn beet red, and then Jon turned his attention to her. "Your first Thanksgiving? Where are you from?"

"Montana," she croaked. *Why* did Jenna have to pull her into this?

"Montana?" She almost laughed at the confused look on Jon's face. It had twisted up like a cartoon character.

"My parents' church banned all holiday celebrations." She dropped her gaze and twisted the rag in her hands that she'd been using to wipe off the island.

No one said anything. She couldn't bring herself to look at them and see the sympathy, or pity, or whatever they were feeling, on their faces. The awkward silence dragged on until the doorbell rang.

"That'll be Pops. I'll get it." Nadia dropped what she was doing and fled the room.

"Pops?" Now it was Josie's turn to look confused.

"That's what Caleb calls his dad," Jon answered her.

"Happy Thanksgiving!" Nadia ushered in what appeared to be an older version of Caleb, with the same black hair but turning gray at the temples. Unlike Caleb's dark eyes, his were blue.

"George, you know my brother Jon. This is Roger's girlfriend, Jenna, and this is Josie. I'm not sure if you met them at the party or not."

"I can't really remember. There were so many people there." He chuckled. "Nice to see you again. Thanks for having me." He handed a basket covered with a kitchen towel to Nadia. "I made my mother's cornbread recipe, as promised."

"Thank you!" She squealed, pulling back the fabric to take a peek. Josie saw fluffy yellow squares poking up from where she sat at the island. "I can't wait. It's the best." She took a deep sniff as she carried it into the dining room.

"So where's Caleb frying this turkey?"

Jenna thumbed toward the backdoor. "Roger and he set it up in the backyard. Can I get you a drink?"

"I'm good for now, thank you. I want to go see how they do this."

"All I know is if it explodes, you're doing it wrong." Josie was the only one who didn't get the joke, as the rest of the room laughed.

As dinner got closer, Josie found herself sitting and observing more than she thought she would. Sam and Frankie turned up with the pies for dessert. The turkey did *not* explode, much to Nadia's chagrin and Caleb's boasting.

When they finally gathered around the dining table, Roger explained that it was a tradition in his family to go around and say one thing they were thankful for this year.

"So since Dad isn't here to start us off, I'll start." Roger cleared his throat, his glass of sparkling wine in his hand. "This year I'm thankful for how my business is growing. Because I get to work with Sam again, and it's because of that job that I found Jenna."

Her friend blushed, which was rare from what Josie had seen so far. "You sap," she teased. "I'm thankful that my dad butted into my life and did something good for once. Even if you were a total pain in my ass at first."

Those in the know laughed as Roger retorted with a fond smile on his face. "Right back atcha, Princess."

Frankie lifted her glass. "I'm thankful for friends who become family."

Sam took his turn. "I'm thankful I won't be working for the government anymore."

Oh crap. Now it was her turn, and all eyes were on her.

"F-freedom," she stammered, looking at her rescuers. They each acknowledged her with either a smile or a nod.

"My son and his future bride." George gestured to Caleb and Nadia.

"That Finn survived," Jon said. It was the most serious he'd been all day.

"That we'll have all of Nadia's brothers with us for the wedding." Caleb placed his hand over Nadia's on the table.

"No longer having the argument about where we're sleeping." Nadia grinned. "And yes, that Finn's alive."

A loud sniff came from the doorway, diverting everyone's attention. Judy and Irving stood there, still wearing their coats.

Nadia took off her glasses and wiped her eyes. "Mom! Dad!"

"Happy Thanksgiving!"

Their children rose to hug them hello. Roger took their coats. Then chairs came up from the basement, plates shuffled around, and all ten of them squeezed around the table.

Dinner might not be as hot as Nadia had intended, but it was still delicious.

After everyone had their plates full, Judy filled them in on Finn's condition.

"They couldn't save his arm. And he may need glasses, they're not sure. It depends on how his eyes heal post-blast. They got most of the shrapnel out of his leg, but not all of it."

"Flying is going to be fun," Jenna commented.

Roger patted her on the shoulder. "The doctor will give him a letter. It'll be fine."

"They said he'll be home next week. I want to throw him a welcome home party."

Roger, Jon, and Nadia all exchanged a look. Nadia was the bravest of them and spoke up. "I don't think that's a good idea, Mom."

"Why not? He deserves it."

"Because he hates being the center of attention?"

Josie could certainly relate to *that*.

"Your brother is coming home, and he deserves a hero's welcome, don't you think?" Judy scooped more mashed potatoes into her mouth as if that ended the discussion. Which it did. Who could argue with that?

"It'll just be at the house. I got the email about his flight information on our way back. It'll just be the family." She started listing off relatives.

"Mom, that's a lot of people," Nadia interjected.

"But they're *family*."

Her other kids shifted uncomfortably in their seats.

Josie wanted to defuse the tension. "Would someone pass the cornbread?"

Finn waited with the rest of the passengers to exit the plane. He could have worn his uniform one last time, but he couldn't stomach the extra attention just to get on and off the plane faster. The stares at his missing arm were bad enough. He didn't need anyone making a fuss over him. Finn wasn't a hero. He'd just been in the wrong vehicle at the wrong time.

All he had with him was his duffle bag, which he'd slung across his chest, but his parents were waiting by the baggage claim to greet him. So that's where he headed. When he saw them, he groaned inwardly.

"Finn!"

Mom waved a big red, white, and blue sign that said "Welcome home" with the Marine Corps insignia on it. Finn gritted his teeth and contemplated pretending he hadn't seen them.

It was like everything he'd told them in Germany had gone in one ear and out the other.

But he didn't have a way to get home otherwise. Plus, she'd already spotted him.

He palmed his face and walked over. "Hi, Mom. Dad."

Mom attacked him with a hug, and he wrapped his left arm around her. "I'm so glad you're home!"

"Please don't cry," he begged her. The last thing he needed was her making a scene at the airport. The poster was bad enough.

She sniffed as she let him go. Dad pulled him into a quick one-armed hug with a pat on his shoulder. "Is that all you brought with you?"

"Yeah, the rest is getting shipped."

"Do you want a drink or anything for the road?"

"No, I'm good." He just wanted to get home and crawl into a hole for a year or two.

Mom filled the drive home with chatter about Nadia's wedding. The way she talked about it, it sounded like *she* was the one getting married, not his little sister.

"Have they picked a date yet?" He asked when he finally got a word in edgewise.

"No, and I'm worried all the venues will be booked! These places book years in advance."

"Now, dear," Dad said from the driver's seat, "they wanted to be sure Finn would be home for it, and you know that's why they haven't set the date yet." Dad gave him an exasperated look in the rearview mirror.

The corner of Finn's lip turned up at that. Of course, Nadia wouldn't set a date until she knew when he'd be home. "I'm sure she'll find something they can both agree on." Most of the venues his mother was talking about weren't Nad's style, anyway. But Finn wasn't going to point that out.

When they turned onto his parents' street, Finn noticed cars parked up and down. "Someone must be having a party."

His mother gave a noncommittal hum. Finn narrowed his eyes at the front passenger seat in front of him. She was up to something.

When they came in sight of the house he'd grown up in, he closed his eyes and leaned back against the seat. "Mom, what did you do?"

The house had red, white, and blue bunting along the porch that his parents usually reserved for Memorial Day and the Fourth of July. A banner spanned the front yard that proclaimed, "Welcome Home, Finn!" for the whole neighborhood to see. Silhouettes crowded the living room windows, showing a house teeming with people.

"I invited the family over for your welcome home party! They're all so happy to see you!"

He had his phone, thanks to his CO. He could order a ride and get the fuck out of there, go to a hotel until the party was over. This was not what he wanted or needed. He'd hoped to come home to a hot meal and a nice nap.

Not small talk and questions he didn't feel ready to answer, not to mention relatives he hadn't seen in ages.

But Mom was so excited, and he knew she'd gone to a lot of trouble to get everybody here on short notice.

He barely registered the chilly December air as he strode for the front door. Best to just get this over with.

Cheers went up when he opened the door. He clenched his jaw and gave them a tight smile even as his ears rang. Thank God his siblings fought to get to the front.

Nadia wrapped her arms around his waist and hugged him fiercely. "I missed you, big brother.""Missed you too, baby sis."

She put her hands on her hip, grunting adorably, and scowled up at him. "That was your only free pass for that." Finn chuckled. Nadia's face fell. "I'm sorry about the party. We tried to talk Mom out of it, but you know how she is when she sets her mind to something…"

"I know." It wasn't his siblings' fault.

Roger and Jon were next in line to hug him hello. "Glad you made it back, Bro."

"Hey." Caleb had come up behind Nadia and handed her a drink. "I saw the video. Good job."

The younger man grinned. "Thanks. I've already asked these two, but I wanted to ask you in person. Would you stand up with me on the big day?"

Caught off-guard, Finn choked on his emotions, trying to control his reaction. "Really?"

"Really. You guys have been there for both of us when it really counted. Plus, I only have one best friend while she's got four." Caleb shrugged. "The math checks out."

Finn gave him a one-armed hug and patted him on the back when he pulled away. "It'd be an honor."

"Mine as well. We're happy to have you back, man." Caleb backed up so he could enter his own party. Roger and Jon flanked Finn as he moved through the house, greeting family members he hadn't seen in ages. Someone handed him a beer. Finally, he leaned against a wall and just tried to breathe.

His brothers formed a human shield around him, as though they'd planned this defense when their mom had gone against his wishes. To be fair, she'd been talking about a much bigger party when they met in Germany, but this was still too much. However, it should be survivable.

After all, he'd survived a fucking bomb.

Chapter 7

THIS PARTY WAS CROWDED as heck. Josie couldn't remember the last time she'd been in a space with this many people per square foot. Maybe one of the christenings at her parents' church? But that felt like another lifetime ago now.

Roger had sworn up and down he'd trust any of these people with his life. They were his family. But Sam and Frankie had agreed to stick close to her.

Frankie was watching some of Roger's relatives school the younger generations in poker and leaning against Sam.

"Sam? I'm going to the kitchen for some water." Honestly, she really needed air. But she wouldn't chance going outside without one of her guards.

"No problem, Josie." He smiled that gentle smile at her. Frankie was lucky. Maybe someday that would be her.

Not until you get your own job and your own place. No more relying on a man.

She squeezed past the other guests on her way to the kitchen. Thank God, it was empty. Josie released her breath and then took another one. She opened the refrigerator and pulled out a bottle of water Mrs. Hunt had stocked especially for the party. They were the cute little sports bottles, with the lids that popped up for drinking.

Despite the cooler December air, the number of bodies in the house meant the air conditioning was on. Josie hadn't been able to feel it out there, but here in the kitchen, the cool air from the vent wafted against her face.

She drank her water and weighed the option of going back out to the game room while she leaned against the counter. Her social battery was swiftly depleting.

Her sanctuary wasn't empty for long. A young guy wearing a long-sleeved Henley slipped into the kitchen from the other door, and leaned against the counter to breathe a sigh, just like she had only a moment ago. He filled out that shirt like no one she'd ever seen before, and Josie felt something she hadn't felt in ages.

Attraction.

He hadn't noticed her yet, just leaned his buzz cut head back against the cabinets, hiding from the chaos on the other side of the doorway. When his head fell forward, she noticed the shadows under his eyes.

"You okay?"

He lifted his head and started to scowl, but it cleared. "Yeah, just tired. Jet lag is a bitch, huh?"

She just smiled. "I imagine so."

He pointed at her water bottle with his left hand. "Where'd you find that?"

"In the fridge." She gestured at the shiny stainless steel appliance.

He headed for it. "Thanks."

Sam appeared at the doorway. "Hey. Frankie's got a headache, so we're heading back to the house. You want a ride?"

She gave him a relieved smile and pushed the top back down on her drink. "Definitely." But she didn't want to be rude. Turning back to the stranger, she gulped when she saw his throat extended as he chugged half of a bottle down. "Have a good night."

He set the bottle down and wiped the back of his mouth with his hand. "You, too."

FINN SLEPT IN FOR the first time in his recent memory, not waking until it was nearly noon. After muddling through his morning routine, made more difficult by the phantom limb that kept reaching for things it couldn't anymore, he pulled on sweats and a t-shirt and went downstairs. He left the stump shrinker sitting on his dresser. The damn thing had driven him crazy yesterday, and his skin itched just thinking about it. Dad made him a sandwich for lunch, and they watched the football game together.

It was exactly what he needed after all the forced socializing the night before.

Somewhere around the third quarter, the telltale scent of Mom's pork chops wafted through the house. By the time the game was over, he was starving.

When they sat down to dinner, Finn's mouth watered at the golden chop and mound of mashed potatoes sitting on his plate. He groaned around a mouthful of potatoes. So much better than hospital food.

The problems came when he had to cut the meat. Food at the hospital had been mushy and easy to cut, but this wasn't. He clenched his teeth as the pork slid around on the plate when he tried to cut it one-handed. Scowling at his dinner, Finn tried putting the fork between his lips so he could hold it in place and cut left-handed. But his hand had started shaking, and he dropped the knife.

Then Mom intervened. "Here, I'll do it." She reached over and plucked the knife and fork away from him, cutting up his dinner like a toddler. Finn's face heated, and he looked away. God, this was embarrassing.

"There you go." She slid the plate back in front of him. Dinner no longer looked as enticing.

"I was figuring it out," he griped. But he took the fork in his left hand and ate it, anyway.

"Once you get the prosthesis, everything will be easier." Her assurances did nothing but remind him of what he'd lost, and the pork turned to ash in his mouth.

He choked down the rest of his dinner and went to put his plate in the dishwasher. "Finn, why don't we play a game? Just the three of us?"

When he used to come back on leave, they often played card games like Uno or Phase 10 after dinner. As his brothers and sister moved out, the games had become smaller, but no less cherished. But how the hell was he supposed to play something like *that*?

"I'm still pretty jet-lagged, Mom. I think I'm just going to go to bed."

"Okay. Don't forget to set an alarm. You have an appointment tomorrow morning at ten with Doctor Lopez."

"Got it." Right. His new prosthetist. Joy. Finn trudged upstairs to shower and sleep.

"How was the party?" Abby asked as she slid into her seat, clipboard in hand.

Josie settled on the couch across from her in the now-familiar office. Pale gray walls with Zen landscape art prints surrounded her. Her therapist appeared to be in her mid-thirties, with shoulder-length dark brown hair. She'd liked her instantly, and not just because she was the only trauma counselor that had had an opening for a new client.

"It was... okay." She took a deep breath. "Tons of people, not a lot of space to move. I only knew the immediate family and Frankie and Sam, of course."

Abby nodded, her pen scratching at the paper. "How long did you stay?"

"About an hour. Frankie got a headache, and since she and Sam were my ride, I left when they did."

"Did it bring up anything for you?"

She shook her head. "Not really. The mood was so different from when I was crowded in captivity. It didn't trigger me."

"Any other recent triggers?"

"I'm still having nightmares occasionally. If I've been cleaning, and I've tired myself out, I don't dream. But when I do dream, I'm back in the syndicate's hold."

"What about the lucid dreaming technique we discussed?"

"It helps sometimes." She licked her lips. "If I become aware I'm dreaming, I can pull myself out now. But if I'm dreaming of being assaulted, I can't."

Abby nodded. "Do you fight back in your dreams?"

"I'm usually pinned down." She trembled, a teardrop smacking down on her arm. Crap, she always ended up crying during these sessions. She reached for a tissue and dabbed at her face.

Abby let her sit with her memories, a technique she'd explained at her first appointment would help her overcome the pain through prolonged exposure. She'd recorded their first session where Josie had recounted her experiences, including the abuse from Brad, and she'd forced herself to listen to them daily for two weeks so she could desensitize herself. That, and the lucid dreaming, had helped a lot. She no longer woke up the whole house with her screams.

She used the breathing techniques that Abby had taught her to bring herself out of the panic attack before it could take hold. *I'm safe,* she reminded herself. *No one here is going to hurt me.*

"Anything else you want to talk about?"

"I hate feeling helpless. It's just sitting back and waiting for the authorities to do something." She dabbed at her eyes again. "I became such a big sister to them, probably because I haven't seen my siblings in so long. And I was a bit older than most of them and had the nursing training."

"And you're worried about them."

"Of course! I can't tell you how many times I begged the customers to use condoms. And good luck getting any medical care. The only time they took us to a clinic was when we got something we could pass on to the clients." She gritted her teeth in anger. "I think one of the girls had a miscarriage. The blood wouldn't stop." Josie shuddered. "When they finally took her to the ER, she was so pale. And then they moved us and I have no idea what happened to her."

Abby said nothing. Josie wasn't sure they'd even taken the poor thing for medical care. She couldn't be sure they hadn't shot her dead and left her body in a ditch, but to be honest, that might have been better.

"I got lucky. So lucky. And I hate myself for it."

"Why?"

"I'm nothing special. Yet because I was unconscious, I have a soft bed, and warm clothes, and food any time I want it."

"And because of you, the authorities are working on getting the whole operation taken down. You've done plenty, Josie. You did things for them when you were in captivity, too. It's not shameful to do things for yourself, now."

"Logically, I know that. And I'm so grateful for the rescue. But I can't help it."

"I think you used your big sister role to compartmentalize your experience. To distract yourself from the trauma. And it's incredible that you were able to do that."

"But I'm not strong enough to get them out."

Abby made another note on her clipboard. "Did you learn about the oxygen mask mentality when you were in nursing school?"

Nursing school felt like a lifetime ago. "I... don't remember."

"In an airplane, when you're flying with a small child, in the event of an emergency, they tell you to put your oxygen mask on first before you place your child's mask on."

"Okay." Where was Abby going with this?

"Because if you black out from lack of oxygen, the child can't put your mask on you. And you might not make it long enough to get the mask on the child. Just because you're putting your proverbial oxygen mask on before going to someone else's rescue doesn't make you weak." Josie thought about that, the silence filling the air. "Another common phrase is, 'You can't pour from an empty cup.'"

That made sense. Josie nodded. "I see." A deep, shuddering breath flowed out of her.

Abby checked the clock on the wall behind Josie and settled back in her chair. "Anything else you want to talk about today?"

"At the party, there was this guy..." She bit her lip. "I don't know his name, but he was so incredibly attractive. And I thought... I didn't think I'd ever be interested in men again."

Abby's eyes widened, a smile spreading across her face. "That's wonderful! What did you talk about?"

Josie shrugged. "I had escaped into the kitchen to get a breather. No one was in there, but he came in from a different room after I did. He looked exhausted and mentioned jet lag. Then he asked about where I found a water bottle, and I showed him." She rolled her now-crumpled tissue in her hand. "It just surprised me."

"If you see him again, would you pursue him?"

Josie shook her head. "After what happened with Brad, I don't want to be in a position where I rely on a man. I need to stand on my own two feet before I trust anyone like that again."

Abby nodded. "That makes sense. We're just about out of time. Let's talk about this at our next session, okay?"

"Okay." Josie wiped her eyes once more and tossed the tissue in the trash can. She knew Roger was waiting for her outside in the special chair the staff had set up for him. Because of her situation, they never made him stay in the public waiting room. "Thanks, Abby."

"Take care, Josie."

Chapter 8

THE NEXT MORNING, HE woke up from a fitful sleep ten minutes before his alarm was set to go off. He sat up in bed and ran a hand—his only hand, now—through his sweaty hair. Ugh, he better hit the shower before he left for the day.

Looking in the mirror, he realized he was starting to look shaggy. His first instinct was to cut it before he returned to base, but he caught himself. There was no going back to base for him.

He clenched his jaw, catching his toothbrush in the middle. Pulling it from his mouth, he spat out the remaining toothpaste and stripped his boxers off. Maybe showering would wash off not just the sweat from the night before, but the foul mood as well.

After wrestling himself into a pair of jeans one-handed, he begrudgingly rolled on his stump shrinker before pulling on a gray long-sleeved Henley. The sleeve swung from his right arm as he descended the stairs, making him wonder if he should put a knot in it or just cut it off.

"Good morning, baby boy." Finn fought hard not to roll his eyes. "I got your favorite."

"Morning, Mom." She slid a bowl of Lucky Charms in front of him, which made him grin. "You probably shouldn't have." He carefully poured the milk in, then lifted his spoon. "But thanks."

"You're welcome." She was eating her own bowl of some kind of flakes with dried strawberries. "Are you looking forward to meeting Doctor Lopez?"

He shrugged. *At least having a fake arm will make it less obvious when I wear long sleeves.*

A pill bottle plopped down in front of him on the table. "You're supposed to take this with food."

Finn sighed. He'd gotten used to ignoring the random twitches from his stump over the last couple of days. It didn't hurt too bad at the moment. "I'm good, Mom." After the appointment would be another story.

She drove him to the Walter Reed Medical Center over in Bethesda, an hour-long drive where she thankfully played the radio and didn't expect him to keep up a conversation. He leaned against the window and watched the scenery go by while he had an argument with himself.

Why did I survive?

Who am I without the Corps?

What the hell do I do now?

His entire adult life and identity was wrapped up in his job as a sniper. As a sophomore, he'd made the varsity rifle team in high school, which was unheard of at the time. They'd traveled to the state competition his senior year, where he took the top score. That's where the Marine recruiter had approached him.

"Quite an impressive score, Mr. Hunt."

"Thank you." Finn eyed the man in camouflage, not quite like his brothers' uniforms. Jon's was the distinctive blue of the Navy, and Roger's was an olive green.

The stranger stuck out his hand. "Corporal Randall Steele. United States Marine Corps."

Finn shook his hand firmly, just like Roger had taught him. "Nice to meet you."

"You ever consider a career in the military?"

Finn shrugged as students, teachers, and parents swarmed around them. They were a boulder in a sea of people. "Sure.

My brothers both serve. Roger's in the Army and Jon's in the Navy. I just hadn't decided where I wanted to go yet."

Corporal Steele produced a business card and held it out to him. "If you decide you want to be one of the few and the proud, give me a call. You could have an amazing career as a sniper."

Finn took the card, slid it into his pocket with a nod. Then he heard his co-captain, Joanna, calling him.

"Hey, Eagle Eye! Coach Atkins said the bus is leaving!"

The reminder of his old nickname, which had followed him into the Marines, sat heavy on his chest. He didn't have his perfect vision anymore, thanks to the bomb. While he didn't need glasses yet, the doctors had warned him he would need them later. The brightness of the blast had strained his eyes and caused them to age faster. Early-onset macular-degeneration, or something.

Leaving Mom in the waiting room of the prosthetist's office, Finn followed the nurse as she took him back to his appointment.

"You're in exam room three today. Sit up here and let me get your vitals."

She took his blood pressure, checked his temperature and his pulse ox, recording the numbers on her computer.

"What's your pain level today?"

Finn shrugged. "Maybe a one." Barely noticeable in comparison, really.

She nodded. "That's good. Doctor Lopez will need you to take this half of your shirt off so she can see the amputation site. And she'll be in with you in a bit." The nurse, probably almost as old as his mother, walked back out of the room and shut the door.

He occupied himself playing a game on his phone, one that Nadia had insisted he download and play with her. She was on level 400-something, but he was catching up quickly. Not like he had anything better to do.

A knock sounded against the door, and Finn yanked his Henley up over the right shoulder just as a petite woman of Hispanic descent entered the room.

"Good morning, Finley. I'm Doctor Lopez. Do you have another name you go by?"

"Call me Finn," he grunted, then remembered his manners. "Nice to meet you."

"It's nice to meet you, too. Let's have a look." She peeled his stump shrinker down and Finn breathed a sigh of relief. "Feels good to take that off, huh?"

"It itches," was all he said as she gently palpated the stump with her small fingers. He had to grit his teeth. Fuck, even that hurt.

"It's not as compressed as I would like. Do you wear the stump shrinker daily?"

He shrugged. "I left it off yesterday."

"It's best to wear it daily so we get a better fit for your prosthesis. The stump will naturally shrink over time, so in order to get the longest life from your prosthesis, we need to shrink it as much as possible before your fitting." She started to manipulate the flesh more, rubbing it in a circle over the incision, and he jumped back at the shooting pain. Doctor Lopez only hummed. "Have you been doing your massages?"

Finn shook his head. "It hurt too much." He'd been trying to do the massages the nurses had taught him in Germany, but it had been so sore and tender any time he touched it, he honestly forgot.

She rolled the stump shrinker back up his arm and sat back on the stool. "Relax, I'm done for now."

He let out a shaky breath, unaware until she mentioned it how his whole body vibrated with tension.

"For maximum comfort, we need the scar tissue to move over the cut bone. I'll leave you with the massage instructions again, and the desensitization instructions. Before you start doing the massages, you'll need to desensitize your stump to touch. Do you towel dry it after a shower?"

He nodded. It tolerated patting with a towel just fine.

"That's good. We can start the fitting process today, but I need you to wear the stump sock daily because it's going to be a part of wearing the prosthesis."

"Isn't it a hook?" His tone gave away his opinions on the fake arms he'd seen before.

She hummed. "There are other options, like myoelectric prosthesis, but they're more expensive and we don't have them here. But that is an option if you want to pursue it. Given how expensive they are, I would wait until the stump is smaller."

"I don't want ... I don't want to lose my biceps." Finn flushed. It was stupid, it was vain, but he wanted to be able to work out again. He'd never forgotten how it felt to leave high school as the scrawny rifle nerd and return with boot camp muscles. The girls who never gave him the time of day in high school had seen him at the mall and the response had been... inspiring. Hadn't he lost enough? "Can I resume my exercise regimen?"

"I'll make a note of it for the technician, but yes, we can give you some attachments that will let you lift again. I just ask that you start out light; don't jump back into your usual routine right away."

He nodded. That all seemed reasonable.

After another nurse came in for his fitting, Finn met his mom in the waiting room. "How did it go?"

"I have to be back in a week." They'd have the prosthesis ready by then. His new arm.

"You hungry?"

"I could eat."

She cocked her head at him. "You want to eat at the cafeteria or somewhere else?"

He shuddered at the thought of more hospital food. "Let's go somewhere else."

They found a tavern that the internet said had amazing burgers on the way back home. When they were escorted to their table, they passed a booth that held four women who appeared to be in their twenties, all dressed up for a night on the town. They gawked at him with appreciation in their eyes. For once, he felt like himself again, and sent them a wink and a cocky grin. The whispered squeals gratified him, but once he turned his back, they saw it.

"Oh my god, what happened to his *arm*?"

"Hush, Brittany!"

His throat was thick as they sat at their table, and his face heated. Eyeing the menu, nothing actually looked good anymore. The girls' reaction to his deformity had stolen his appetite.

Chapter 9

JOSIE STARED AT HERSELF in the mirror. Her cheeks had finally filled out, and her skin no longer sagged. Her blonde hair had soaked up the conditioner she'd been using regularly and the dark circles under her eyes were gone. She looked... *healthy*.

Looking into a mirror was no longer a jarring prospect. Sure, she was still thin, and there were days she worried her appetite might never go back to normal, but she was bouncing back much easier than she would have thought.

It's these amazing people I've found, she thought to herself. *They've just accepted me like I've always been here.*

She shook her head and got back to cleaning the powder room. If she thought about it too long, she'd cry.

The one place she didn't clean was Roger's office. He'd asked her to let him take care of it, because of the nature of his work. She completely understood.

A knock came on the open bathroom door. "Josie?"

She paused with the toilet brush in her hand. "What's up, Roger?"

He sighed, wiping a hand over his face. "I need a favor."

Her heart leaped at the chance to be useful and pay him back for everything he, Jenna, Frankie, Sam, and Nadia had done for her these past weeks. "What do you need?"

"You know how my little brother lost his arm?"

She nodded, guilt creeping in. They'd invited her to the welcome home party, but she didn't have the energy that day to deal with crowds, so she'd hid in the kitchen. When Sam and Frankie had to leave early, she caught a lift home. She'd hardly stayed an hour.

"My mom called me. Apparently, she's at her wits' end with him. He's not taking care of the stump like he's supposed to, and now he's shouting at her and she doesn't know what to do. I wanted to ask you if you would mind if I brought him here. Mom has a tendency to hover, and that's not what he needs right now." She turned the brush around in her hands. The only other guest room at

Roger's house was the one that shared a bathroom with hers. Frankie and Sam had been staying there until a few days ago, when they went to Denver, so Sam could pack up his apartment and move to Baltimore. They'd already signed the lease on an apartment, which meant the room was free.

"Does he know about me?"

"Probably not. I won't tell him anything you're not comfortable with. But I swear he won't be a threat to you. And if he makes you uncomfortable at any point, I can still beat the shit out of him."

She couldn't suppress the giggle that bubbled up out of her at his fierce expression.

"I'm serious."

"I know." Josie bit her lip. That didn't seem like an actual favor. "Was that all?"

"You're a nurse, right?"

"Not technically," she sighed. "I never got to take the boards." Which she was studying for again. She didn't want to sit for them until this mess with the syndicate and FBI wrapped up, but her skills needed the refresher course, anyway.

"I know you're not licensed, but you're always worried about 'paying me back,' and all that nonsense." He put finger quotes around those three words and she grinned shyly. "But if you could take point on his home care... that would help us out a lot. Mom's trying, but it comes across as her babying him, and it's not going over well."

"No, I imagine it wouldn't." A big, badass Marine reduced to his mommy taking care of him? Yeah, she couldn't see it either.

"But you don't have history with him. It's almost like having a home health nurse come. Plus, it would give you some practice. I'd be happy to write a reference letter when it comes time for you to hunt for a job."

"I'll see what I can do. But I don't know that he'll let me help him, either. Because he doesn't know me, and I'm not really a nurse."

"If it doesn't work, I'll find something else. But I gotta get him out of that house or they're going to drive each other nuts."

"I'll do my best. What kind of amputation was it?"

"Below the elbow. On his dominant side."

"Okay." Her mind whirled. She had access to a virtual library thanks to an account Roger had set up under his name. She'd start researching there. "I'll take a look at his paperwork when you can get him here."

"Thanks, Josie. You're a lifesaver."

She shook her head. "Don't be silly. It's the least I can do." She paused. Now that she had him here, she had to ask. "Any word from the FBI?"

"Nothing yet. I'll have Sam reach out."

"Thanks. I'm so worried about those girls. The syndicate didn't always keep them. So the faster they get out..." Her voice trailed off as she bit her bottom lip.

"I know. I wish I knew more, Josie." He gave her a sad smile and squeezed her shoulder. "Tell Jenna I'll be back for dinner. I gotta rescue Mom."

Finn wanted to throw the stump sock against a wall. Or burn it. He wanted to climb into a hole and never come out.

Nothing was ever going to be the same. All of his dreams were gone.

Those girls weren't the only ones that had stared at his lack of an arm. And it would happen everywhere he went. His little pipe dream of the wife, the house, the picket fence, and the kids? It had blown up with his unit.

No one would want a broken ex-sniper. He had no job skills, no future. How the hell could he even *fuck* with one arm?

He'd drawn the shades tight against the late afternoon sun and shut off all the lights. When he'd gotten home, he'd pawed through his closet and rediscovered his old boom box and the CD collection he'd amassed before enlisting.

Finn cranked the volume up to eleven. He just wanted to forget everything. He wanted to go numb.

That was hours ago. When Roger burst through his door and turned off the music, the silence was deafening.

"Linkin Park? Really? What are you, in high school?"

"Can't you knock?" Finn growled from the bed.

"I did. Not that you could have heard me." Roger shut the door behind him and leaned against it, crossing his arms over his chest. "I don't think you could even hear yourself think with it that loud."

"That was the fucking point," he muttered.

"What was that?"

"I said, fuck off!"

Roger shook his head, the bastard. "No can do, little Bro. I think you should come with me."

"What are you talking about?"

"Mom's worried, and I know her hovering is driving you up a wall."

Okay, he wasn't wrong.

"Frankie and Sam got an apartment and they're not staying with me anymore. So there's space for you at my place, and Mom won't be around twenty-four-seven like she is here." Finn contemplated this. He didn't want to admit it, but Roger's idea was solid.

"What's the catch?"

"The catch is Josie."

"Josie?"

"Okay, she's not a catch exactly, but she *is* staying with me and Jenna while she's under Hunt Security's protection."

A client? Okay, Finn could deal with that.

"I need you to be nice to her. Also, you'll have to share a bathroom with her, so be conscious of that."

Finn sat up, eyeing his oldest brother warily. "Who is she? Besides a client?"

"That's not my story to tell. If she wants to tell you, she will. All I can say is we're her protection."

"Alright. Let me pack up my clothes."

"I'll help. There's a brand-new mattress with your name on it."

Packing went quickly with Roger's assistance, and then Finn found himself standing in front of his parents.

"I'm going to stay with Roger for a bit." He couldn't look his parents in the eyes. While he hated the way he'd been acting, he couldn't stop it either. "I'm... I'm sorry. I'm not good company right now."

"You can tell us anything, Finn. We love you." Mom stood there with worry written all over her face, but no. He couldn't talk to her about this. He didn't talk about feelings.

Dad reached over and grasped his shoulder. "Take some time with your brother, son. It's hard to feel like an adult when you're staying with your parents." He nodded and followed Roger out to his Chevy Silverado.

On the drive over to his place, Roger had the stupidest idea Finn had ever heard.

"You know, when you're healed up, maybe you'd be interested in taking security jobs with me?"

Finn scoffed. "I can't even drive my own truck. This new arm they're giving me is going to have a hook. There's no way I could fire a gun."

Roger hummed. "You never know. Technology's pretty amazing."

But he would rather talk about anything but his own problems. "Why is Josie staying with you? Shouldn't you be guarding her at her place?"

"It's easier this way. I have cameras all around the property, and an alarm system most people don't. I tried to get Jenna to stay with me instead of in that shitty apartment when I was her bodyguard, but she's stubborn as hell."

The corner of Finn's mouth lifted despite his sour mood. "She's perfect for you, then."

"Damn straight."

They pulled onto Roger's long-ass gravel driveway and Finn took in the two-story farmhouse Roger had bought for himself, a single guy. It was eerily similar to what Finn had dreamed about purchasing. He had saved most of his money while he was a Marine, and now that he was almost certain to remain single forever, he wasn't ready to give up on the house dream.

Maybe not a big one, he thought to himself. *Just two bedrooms, so I have a workout room and some land to call my own.*

He could finish the basement to look like a tavern and have his brothers and sister over to play *Dungeons and Dragons.*

Finn's daydream was interrupted when they pulled into Roger's detached garage and shut off the truck.

"I meant it about Josie. You upset her, and you're going right back to Mom and Dad's."

"I hear you." Finn raised his hand. The phantom limb he'd been warned about raised its head too, and he felt like he was lifting both of them, but he knew it wasn't true. Ugh, that was weird.

"Alright, let's go see what the girls want to do for dinner."

Finn followed Roger up to the front door, and through it, carrying his bag of clothes. Jenna came thumping down the stairs. "Hey!"

"Hey, little Amazon." Roger leaned down and gave her a firm kiss on the mouth. Finn had to turn his head. But when he did, he spied the most beautiful woman he'd ever met.

Tall and willowy, with pale blond hair like butter, and the biggest gray eyes he'd ever seen. She was just wearing leggings and a long t-shirt, but she walked down the stairs with a captivating elegance. He briefly remembered meeting her in the kitchen at his parents' party, but he hadn't been paying enough attention.

He was paying attention now.

"Hello."

"Hello." Finn cleared his throat. He sounded like he'd been chewing the gravel outside.

"Finn, this is Josie. She's staying with us. Josie, this is my little brother, Finn."

"Nice to meet you." Her voice floated on the air. He could listen to her read the dictionary.

"Nice to meet you, too." Finn was rather grateful she didn't reach out to shake his hand, because that would have been awkward.

Because his right hand, the one you shook in greeting, was gone.

His gaze dropped back to the floor as he realized this angel would never look at him that way. He'd better get used to being alone.

Chapter 10

THE FIRST THING JOSIE noticed about Roger's brother was his absolutely gorgeous face. The second was that he was the guy she'd met in the kitchen at the party. His reddish-brown hair that he shared with his siblings was cut close to his head, and his skin was still a bit tanned from being in the desert, which made his pale green eyes even more arresting. She'd overheard Roger telling Jenna this brother was ten years younger than him, but this guy barely looked twenty-five, not in his thirties.

He had a couple of inches on Roger, and clearly he worked out a *lot.* Her mouth went dry when she spied those biceps hidden by his gray Henley. Yeah, a guy like this wouldn't take kindly to his mom trying to baby him.

When he dropped his gaze, she shook herself free of his mesmerizing presence.

"What do you want to do for dinner?" Roger asked Jenna.

"Honestly, I just want to order pizza if that's okay."

"Sounds good. Meat lovers for me and Finn, and whatever you girls want."

"Josie, what do you like on your pizza?"

Her mouth watered at the mere suggestion. Oh God, when was the last time she'd had pizza? Before ... everything. When Brad still acted like he cared once in a while.

Then she realized everyone was waiting for her.

"Um, mushroom? I'm not really picky."

"How do you feel about spinach?"

She nodded. "I like it."

"Okay, mushroom and spinach for us, and heart attack in a box for the boys." Jenna finished typing into her phone and clicked a button. "Okay, it'll be here in forty."

"That's plenty of time for me to help you get your shit upstairs."

"I got it," Finn grunted, moving away from Roger's outstretched hand and moved past Josie onto the stairs.

"Let me show you to your room." Roger's exasperation came through in his tone, and he gave Josie and Jenna a resigned look as he followed his brother.

"Boys." Jenna rolled her eyes, and Josie had to chuckle.

She followed Jenna into the kitchen, and found herself staring back at the hall, waiting for Finn to come back down. *No! You dummy, he's practically your patient*, she told herself. No matter how hot he was, he was off-limits. Besides, after Brad, she knew she had terrible taste in men. And if something happened between her and Roger's brother, there was no doubt in her mind that Roger would take his side when it fell apart. Nope, it was independence or bust for her.

When their pizza arrived, Roger and Finn came back downstairs. Roger handed the delivery person his cash and carried the boxes into the kitchen. Jenna had set the island with four plates, and was busy getting drinks.

"Water for me, Jenna."

"Just a Coke, thanks." Finn responded.

The boys attacked their pizza piled with pepperoni, sausage, beef, and grease, Finn wolfing down two slices before she even ate half of one.

"So, Josie, what do you do while you're cooped up in here?"

Josie nearly choked on her pizza when she realized Finn was talking to *her*. His intense gaze had her feeling that the heat was turned up too high. Ugh, did he have to be so hot?

"I've been cleaning and studying.""You're in school?"

"No, I have my nursing degree, but I have to sit for the NCLEX so I can get my license. I'm just studying to refresh my memory." When she'd finished speaking, Finn's expression fell into a glower. At first, she thought it was for her, and her sharp intake of breath was the only sign of her fear. But then he turned it on Roger. It was subtle, as she'd figured out he wasn't very expressive, but the temperature of the room dropped right back down to freezing.

After an awkward moment while the two brothers had a silent argument between the two of them, Jenna broke the ice, bless her. She tapped Roger on the shoulder. "Hey, babe, it's December. When are we getting a tree?"

A tree? A *Christmas* tree? Josie forgot all about the dark cloud hanging over the kitchen as she thought about getting to decorate her very first Christmas tree.

"I always go to my parents' house, so I don't bother with a tree."

"Seriously? No way, mister, we're getting a tree." Jenna gave him the side eye. "Do you at least decorate outside?"

He shrugged and chewed the bite of pizza in his mouth. "Who's going to see it?"

"We will! Ugh, men." Jenna shook her head and Josie held back her laugh. "We're getting a tree. And ornaments. And lights. And we're going to decorate the shit out of this huge ass house."

"Whatever you want, Princess." Roger had a fond smile on his face. "You'll bully me into it, so might as well just give in now."

That's when Jenna pouted and leaned forward. "I was looking forward to convincing you tonight."

"I won't say no to that." Roger wagged his eyebrows at her.

Josie blessed her earplugs and wondered if Finn had brought any. From the groan he made, she suspected not.

"I don't want to hear it, you two."

Jenna just stuck her tongue out at him, and Josie resolved to offer him a pair before they went to bed. After all, if he couldn't get a good night's sleep, he would have a much harder time healing. And he *was* her patient, of sorts.

LATE THAT NIGHT, WHEN Roger went upstairs to shower, Finn caught him in the hall.

"What the ever lovin' *fuck*, Roger?" He whispered sharply, wary of someone overhearing. But the girls were downstairs watching a Christmas movie on TV and they shouldn't hear anything.

He turned from his bedroom door, raising an eyebrow at Finn. "What's wrong?"

"What's wrong? You got me here under false pretenses!"

"And how did I do that?"

How dare he be this calm? Finn wasn't the unreasonable one here. "You never said she was a nurse!"

"You didn't ask."

"I don't need a nurse. That's why Mom was driving me crazy."

"You might not need a nurse, but you do need someone that doesn't have an emotional interest in your health to kick your ass and get you to take care of yourself. The fact she's had professional training is a bonus." Roger held up a hand and Finn fumed, but stayed silent. "It was the only way to get Mom to calm down and give you both space. You don't know Josie, she doesn't know you. It's just like having one of those home health nurses come here, except she's already staying here, anyway."

That reminded Finn she wouldn't just be down the hall. She'd be next door, sharing a bathroom with him.

"At least the view will be better when she's reminding you to take your pills." Roger chuckled. "I saw the way you were looking at each other at dinner."

"I don't need to be *babied*."

"Good thing she's not our mother, then." Roger's gaze sharpened, his voice deepening to a growl.

"What's in it for her?" Finn refused to back down. He'd come here to lick his wounds and hide out, but now he was faced with temptation on a stick and told she was supposed to be his nursemaid? He could have ignored her, but not now.

"She needs the practice. I want to help her rebuild her self-confidence. You only think your life is over. She's starting over with *nothing*." Roger stabbed his finger in Finn's chest as he leaned in to make his point.

The words tried to penetrate Finn's hard outer shell, but he wouldn't let them.

Roger wiped a hand over his face. "I can't tell you any more than that. It's her story to tell, if she wants to trust you with it. But if you upset her, you are back at Mom and Dad's house. Hunt Security is all she's got."

Finn stayed in the hall after Roger shut the door, still fuming. He walked across the hall to his guest room and slammed the door shut. Sitting on the edge of his bed, he set his elbows on his thighs, but quickly lifted the right one as a stab of pain echoed up to his shoulder. Fuck, he couldn't even brood properly anymore. Leaning against the left elbow, he laid his head in his hand.

Josie's laugh floated up the staircase. Something funny must have happened on the screen. He pictured it, her head of pale corn silk hair cascading down her back, gray eyes sparkling. Her speaking voice was light as air, and her musical laugh... went straight to his cock.

Groaning, he fell back on the bed, hardening in the athletic pants he'd been living in while at home. In his mind's eye, he saw her, that shy smile she'd used at dinner, aimed at him and only him. He cupped himself through his pants. She seemed so innocent, while he was not. He had blood on his hands, even if he'd been under orders for every kill. Josie reminded him of sunshine. Not the bright beam of the summer, but the little peek you got in winter, when all you wanted was to coax it out. And when that sun finally shone on you, it felt glorious.

It almost seemed wrong to rub one out while thinking of his ray of sunshine. Especially when he was far too broken and dirty to do anything in real life with her. Roger said she was starting over. She needed a man that had all his limbs functioning, one that wasn't damaged by war and loss. That dream of mowing the lawn and going into the house to see his wife came back to him.

He had both arms in it, could touch her, love her the way she deserved. The wife he'd never really seen details of took on Josie's form.

"Lawn's done, baby." Finn slid his body between her and the island.

"I can smell that," she said, waving her hand in front of her nose. "You need a shower, mister."

He grabbed onto her hips and pressed kisses down her neck. "Why don't you join me?"

Hot water streamed down her smooth pale skin, contrasting against his hands tanned in the sun. Soaping up his hands and washing her all over, only to cup her breasts and make her moan and writhe against him. Pushing her against the slick tile as he slid into the slickness between her thighs...

Finn grunted as he came into his hand. He'd snuck his hand down to jerk off without even thinking about it. The orgasm relaxed him, but it faded quickly as the guilt set in. She probably thought of him as nothing more than a practice patient to get her feet wet for a real job. And here he was lusting after her like a jarhead who hadn't gotten laid in... okay, it *had* been a long time. But that was no excuse.

He got up and went into the bathroom to clean up, rinsing the evidence down the sink and letting the water run so she wouldn't know what he'd done.

Because it would never happen for real.

Chapter 11

THE NEXT MORNING, ROGER handed Josie a cup of coffee and the creamer Jenna liked. "Finn isn't happy with me."

"I'm sorry." Josie doctored her coffee and took a sip. "Do you want to talk about it?"

"I do. Because unfortunately, it involves you." Roger ran a hand through his chestnut hair and refused to meet her gaze. "I, uh, wasn't entirely open with him when I suggested he come stay with me."

Josie furrowed her brows. "What do you mean?"

He took a sip of his coffee. "I didn't tell him you were a nurse." He winced. "And now he's pissed."

"Well, technically I'm not. I don't have my nursing license. So you didn't really lie to him."

"No, but I neglected to mention you were going to help with his care."

"He's a grown man. I didn't think I'd need to do much. He's probably capable of taking care of it himself."

"Yeah, that's the thing. He *is* capable, but he isn't doing what the doctor suggested." Roger scrubbed a hand over his face. "Mom told me there are massages and stuff he's supposed to do, but he doesn't do them. That she saw the notes when he came home from the doctor that says he's not." Roger set the mug down on the island. "And she says he doesn't enjoy taking his pain pills."

Josie nodded. "Patients often complain about the side effects of narcotics. Stomach aches, wooziness... Maybe there's something over the counter he can take?"

Roger gestured at the medicine cabinet. "He's welcome to whatever I have in there. Something's better than nothing." He adjusted his sleeves, and Josie noticed for the first time he was wearing a dress shirt. "I have to run out to meet with a client, but Jenna's here. I should be back around lunchtime."

"Have a good meeting." Josie sipped at her coffee while he left through the front door. It occurred to her too late to ask Roger what time Finn woke up. Although she guessed since he wasn't in the Marines anymore, he might like to sleep in.

She knew she certainly would.

So Josie made herself some breakfast, checked on Jenna, who was in Roger's office sorting paperwork, and sat down to study the NCLEX books Jenna had been nice enough to order online for her. She'd promised to pay her back, and though Jenna waved her off when she'd mentioned it, she had a list of things she wanted to pay them back for once she got a job. But in order to do that, she had to pass the test.

By the time she came up for air, the clock on the mantle read eleven-thirty. And there had been no sign of life from the guest room on the other side of her bathroom.

She didn't feel right going up there to wake him as if she were his mother. But that's when the doorbell rang.

Jenna stomped down the steps like a herd of mustangs, her phone in her hand. "It's Judy, nothing to worry about," she said to Josie. Ah. Roger and Finn's mother.

Jenna let Judy into the front hall. "I just wanted to drop this off for Finn. It came in the mail today, overnighted from Bethesda. It should be his new arm." She gazed around the room, taking in Josie on the couch in her sweep. "Isn't he here?"

"Hey, Finn!" Josie swore the walls rattled from Jenna's shout. "You up?"

"I am *now*," he growled. A door opened upstairs. She heard the rustle of fabric, and then Josie's mouth dried completely up when Finn appeared at the top of the stairs, shirtless.

She was so distracted by the peaks and valleys that were his muscles that she didn't even miss his right arm, or the fact he wasn't wearing his stump sock.

"Finley Michael! You're supposed to be wearing that shrinker!"

He palmed his face, still groggy with sleep. "I just woke up, Mom."

"It's nearly noon!"

He clenched his jaw so hard Josie swore he was going to crack a tooth. His next words were a growl. "What do you *want*?"

Judy huffed and held out a box. "Your arm came in the mail. I thought you might want it."

When Finn didn't come down the stairs, Jenna took the box from her outstretched arms. "Thanks, Judy. We appreciate you running it over. Did you want to stay for lunch?"

"No, I have my lunch with the church ladies for our monthly meeting. But thank you, Jenna, that's very sweet." She glared up at her son in the way only a mother could get away with. "I'll see you all later. Have a good day."

The door shut behind her and Finn visibly relaxed, breathing easier.

"I thought they usually brought you in for an appointment when a prosthesis came in," Josie offered as she stood from the couch.

Jenna shrugged, and so did Finn. "I have P.T. Friday. I guess I'll take it with me."

"Oh good. They can show you how to maneuver with it."

He disappeared back into his room, and Jenna laid the box on the coffee table. The look she gave Josie communicated exactly what Josie had been thinking. *What the hell was that?*

Finn, his shirt and stump sock on, came back down the stairs, a pile of papers in his hands. He laid them out next to the box and flipped through them with his one hand. "Ah. There's a note that I'm supposed to bring it with me to my next appointment, but not to try it on until then." He left his papers on the table and walked toward the kitchen. That's when Josie noticed that it also had notes about his stump shrinker.

She cleared her throat. "It also mentions wearing the shrinker daily or you won't be able to wear the arm."

The glare he shot at her over his shoulder would make most men and women wilt. But Josie had endured far worse this past year. It didn't faze her one bit.

His stump sock hung from his arm instead of cupping his limb like it should. Obviously he had trouble pulling it up with only one hand. As Jenna pulled out sandwich fixings for lunch, Josie followed him into the kitchen.

"Would you like a hand to pull it up tighter?"

He sneered at her, and she wondered how she could still find him handsome even now. "What do you know about it? Do you have experience in limb care?"

"No, but I am a nurse."

"A nurse without a license."

If he thought he could drive her away this way, he was wrong. "No, I don't have my license yet, but I *have* the training, and *way* too much time on my hands. Time I've been using to research amputations in the most recent medical journals through the library."

He fell into a sullen silence, but his gaze never left her.

"My only point was, it's difficult to pull the shrinker up one-handed and it can't be comfortable like that."

"It's not comfortable, period."

"Finn! Be nice." Jenna slapped the lunch meat container down on the counter. "She is offering you help."

"Because Roger told her to."

"No, he asked. And I said I would. But I'm not going to touch you without asking first."

Finn's chin dropped, and his eyes shut. "Okay."

"What was that?" Jenna's sharp voice cut through the tension.

"Please."

Josie reached out a hand and slipped her fingers between his warm skin and the tight compression sock. "I'll just be your extra hand. You know how hard you can stand to pull on it."

Slowly he reached up and grabbed the other side, then started to pull. She matched his pace, pulling the sock up evenly so it sat where it was supposed to.

"Thanks," he muttered as Jenna slid a sandwich and chips in front of him.

"You're welcome." She boldly took the stool next to him, though she noticed he always sat on the end so no one could sit next to his arm. "Is it still sensitive?"

He nodded.

"Have they gone over the desensitization process with you?"

Finn sighed as he answered. "Yes."

"How's that going?" She was being cheeky on purpose, testing him while Jenna was in the room.

"It's not," he growled.

"Well, let me know if you want some help with that. Or with the massages they want you to do." She swallowed her nerves at touching a man again. It was different this time, a professional capacity. But as much as she told herself that, it was hard not to remember the things she'd been forced to do by the syndicate.

As a nurse, I have to touch all my patients, and not just the female ones, she told herself.

Roger thought she was doing him a favor, but in reality, this would be helpful for her as well.

FINN DIDN'T TURN INTO the magical, perfect patient in the next two days. That night, Josie listened for the telltale sound of water running in their shared bathroom. When ten o'clock came and went, and she still hadn't heard anything, she went knocking on the door between the bathroom and Finn's bedroom.

"Yeah?"

She opened the door and leaned against the doorjamb. "Just wanted to know when you plan to take your shower?"

Finn raised an eyebrow behind the book he had propped up on his legs. "What's it to you?"

"Well, we share a bathroom, and I didn't want to hog all the hot water." Crossing her arms over her chest, she held herself together. Josie hated confrontation, but for all practical purposes, this was her patient, and she needed to treat him accordingly.

He scoffed and made a point to ignore her. But he didn't turn the page. "Not much point to showering, is there?"

"Your instructions said to keep the site clean, you have to shower daily."

"I haven't gotten it dirty."

Her eyes caught on the stump shrinker on the nightstand. "When's the last time you washed the sock?"

"I don't know."

Probably never, Josie thought to herself. Since he wasn't going to do it, she marched over to the nightstand and snatched it off the top.

"Hey!"

"You're supposed to wash it every other day or you're risking an infection." Josie left the door to the bathroom open so he could watch what she was doing. Hand soap wasn't ideal, but it would do.

She filled the sink with hot soapy water and swished the stump shrinker around. Then she rinsed it twice and squeezed the water out of it. A quick dive into her closet revealed a clip hanger, which would work to let it air dry.

Clipping it up, she hung it off the doorknob on the inside of Finn's room. She nearly gasped, but managed to swallow it in time. Finn had risen off the bed and stood in the doorway, glowering at her.

"I can do that."

"Well, I was right there." She gave him her best wide-eyed stare. "Now, do you need help in the shower?"

"*No!*"

This time, she couldn't help but jump back at his tone. Her heart fluttered in her throat. "Just thought I'd check. I'll leave you to it." She exited back into her bedroom and shut the door. Leaning against it, she held her breath until she heard him start the water with an exasperated sigh. *Phew.*

No wonder Judy had complained to Roger.

Chapter 12

"GOOD MORNING!" BRIGHT LIGHT pierced Finn's eyelids, startling him out of a dead sleep.

"Mmph," he grunted. "What time is it?"

Josie's voice greeted his ears. "It's nine o'clock, and your brother is very kindly making breakfast."

Finn groaned and turned, burying his face in the pillow.

"Come on, up and at 'em! You need to clock more time in the stump shrinker for Doctor Lopez."

He furrowed his brows as he recalled how that sassy little thing had washed the stupid sock for him. It hadn't even registered as something he'd need to do, mostly because he hadn't wanted to acknowledge its existence.

"I could throw some cold water on your face."

That did it. "Fine! I'm getting up, woman." Finn threw off the covers. His arm thumped this morning. The pain had apparently killed his morning wood, although if she'd gotten an eyeful it would serve the little she-devil right.

When he sat up in the bed, her back was to him. He tried not to think about why that disappointed him.

She squeezed the little torture device the doctor insisted he wear. "Looks like your stump shrinker is dry. Why don't I help you with that now and you can get dressed when I leave?"

"Fine," he growled. He eyed her as she strode across the room. She was dressed for comfort in leggings and a sweatshirt. Meanwhile, he was in his underwear, but that didn't seem to faze her. She wasn't looking down.

He grumbled as she pulled the stump sock up tight.

"See you downstairs!" She waved with a grin and the door to his room shut behind her.

With a groan, Finn pushed up from the bed and headed to the bathroom to take care of business. He contemplated shaving his face while he brushed his teeth. It wasn't that bad, yet. He'd shaved before getting on the flight home. And it would take forever to do one-handed.

His stomach rumbled. Maybe Roger had finally perfected Mom's pancake recipe. Not that pancakes from a box would be bad. But that had been his favorite growing up. He missed those lazy pancake Saturdays from when he was a kid. The memories were fuzzy, but he knew they'd happened. Once Nadia had come along, Mom had been too busy and pancake Saturdays had fallen by the wayside.

He clumsily pulled his clothes on one-handed, then jogged down the stairs barefoot. The scent of bacon cooking lured him to the kitchen just as Roger set a plate piled high with it on the kitchen island.

Jenna and Josie sat around, eating plates of fluffy scrambled eggs. Finn's shoulders slumped.

"Morning, little brother. What's wrong?"

"Nothing." But Finn didn't even sound convincing to himself as he pulled out a seat and slid onto it.

Roger placed a plate in front of him. "I've got more eggs coming up. Do you want cheese in them?"

"Sure." He snagged a few pieces of bacon off the serving plate and munched. That's when he saw the bottle of pain pills by his place. Subtle.

"Here you go." Finn leaned back as Roger shoveled scrambled eggs off the skillet and onto his plate. "Seriously, what's wrong?"

Finn tried to dance around the subject. "Do you have Mom's pancake recipe?"

Roger shook his head as he plated his own food. "I've tried to make it. But they never come out right."

"I miss pancake Saturdays from when I was a kid."

"Wow." Roger scrubbed a hand over his face. "I haven't thought about those in ages.""Pancake Saturdays?" Jenna asked, raising her coffee mug to her lips.

"Yeah. Some Saturdays Mom would make pancakes for breakfast." Roger turned back to Finn. "Dude, that was like, before Nadia was born."

Finn just shrugged and shoveled eggs into his mouth. Pancakes were a bad idea anyway, now that he thought about it. He'd need a knife, and it'd be the pork chops all over again.

"Is my cooking that bad?" Roger asked.

Finn swallowed his eggs quickly so he could speak. "What? No!"

"You're scowling at them."

"It's nothing." He glanced away.

Josie shifted in her seat. "I suggested eggs because the protein will help with your healing. I thought Roger would know if you liked them or not."

Finn shook his head. "It's fine." Oh, that came out harder than he wanted it to. Thankfully, everyone left him alone after that. They talked about Jenna's friend Frankie and Roger's friend Sam heading back to Denver to pack up his apartment. Roger suggested Jenna go to the range while he worked at home so she could get used to her new sidearm. Apparently she was going to work for his security company.

It just served to remind him he'd never fire a gun again. Regardless of whether he had a hook or a fake hand, he simply couldn't see a solution.

That part of his life was over.

He barely tasted his breakfast as it went down his gullet. When he got up to go back upstairs to do... something, Roger called out.

"Hey man, you forgot your pill!"

The dull ache in his stump throbbed in time with his pulse. "Don't need it.""You sure, man?"

"Yes," he gritted out. Didn't his brother think he knew his own mind?

"Alright." He could hear the defensiveness in Roger's tone, like he had his hands in the air. Silence descended over the kitchen, and Finn fled the room.

Josie TRIED TO REMIND herself that any progress was better than nothing, even if it had been mere inches over the past couple of days. Finn's mood swings went from bad to worse, and in just forty-eight hours, he'd managed to alienate his brother and Jenna so badly that they were out on a date night.

And they'd left her with him.

"Ross is outside keeping guard if anything happens," Roger assured her. "He's not on the clock or here officially; this is his free time. But he understands I couldn't leave you unguarded."

"Thanks, Roger. I'm sure we'll be fine," she'd said.

But that was an hour ago.

After his shower, Finn begrudgingly agreed to let her try some of the desensitization on his stump. That's why they sat on his bed, with him still damp with water and various textures that she was about to try on his most sensitive area.

Well, the most sensitive area that was appropriate.

She took the cotton ball and gently rubbed it over his skin, starting at the top of his arm and traveling down. He shivered as she got to the very end and rubbed in circles over where his elbow used to be.

"How's that feel?"

"Kinda... tickles."

"Shall I move on to something else?"

"Sure."

Well, at least this wasn't a patient who'd talk your ear off. She set the cotton ball down and picked up the t-shirt, and went through the same motions. His brow furrowed, but he didn't say anything or show any outward signs of pain.

"How's that?"

"It's fine."

Josie wasn't sure, but he made a motion with his hand that meant he wanted her to hurry up, so she dropped the shirt and reached for the towel.

She must not have spent enough time rubbing it on the upper part of the arm, because when she rubbed over the stump, he hissed. Dropping the towel, she raised both hands to show there was no more coming. "Not good?"

"No," he gritted through his teeth.

"What's your pain level?"

He thought about it for a minute. "Five.... It feels like the towel's still there."

"I promise it's not touching you." She waited for a minute, then when his face didn't relax, she decided to try something else. "Do you want a pain pill?"

"No!" His shout took her off guard and made her heart beat faster in her chest. He leaped from the bed and paced, towering over her and making her feel small while he screamed. "Why is it everyone thinks the answer is a fucking pill? I *hate* those things and no one. Shuts. Up. About. The. God. Damn. Pills!"

Josie jumped, falling to the floor, her entire body trembling. Her breaths shortened, the bedroom fell away, and she was back in the crappy apartment she'd shared with Brad. He was screaming at her about something she'd done or not done. Whichever it was, it didn't matter. All that mattered was he was going to raise his hand to her, and she couldn't go back to class with bruises again. She'd have to skip class and her whole life, her freedom was *riding* on this! Her muscles tensed as she raised her hands over her head to protect her face. If the bruises weren't on her face, she could still escape for class.

"Josie, Josie! I'm sorry. I-I didn't mean to scare you." A hand laid on her back and she wigged out.

"Don't touch me!" She shrieked, tears running down her face. The hand disappeared. "Don't touch me."

"Okay, okay. I won't. But I'm not... Josie, I'm not mad at you. I wouldn't ever... Jesus, I would never hurt you. Please, Josie, I'm sorry. Come back."

That didn't sound like Brad, or one of the syndicate's customers. They never stopped when she asked. The blue carpet of the room came into view. Roger's house. She was in Roger's house. Josie noticed her frantic breaths, and she struggled to slow them down.

Suddenly Finn was on the floor with her, breathing with her. "In, and out. Nice and slow." She blinked, her vision clearing. "There you are."

"I, uh, I..." Josie sat up, shame heating her cheeks, which she was sure were red as a Santa suit.

"I'm sorry," they said at the same time.

Staring at each other, it struck Josie that she had to look a fright, and the thought of Finn witnessing her freak out was worse than the panic attack itself. "I'm just going to go." Ignoring his outstretched hand, she rose to her feet. When she was sure they wouldn't give out on her, she bolted through the bathroom into her room and shut the door behind her. Keeping her back against it, she slid down to the floor and cried silent tears of shame.

This. *This* was why she could never trust a man again.

Chapter 13

Finn collapsed on his bed, staring at the door to Josie's room, his pain forgotten. He scrubbed his hand over his face as his chest tightened in a vise grip. Roger hadn't hinted at anything in Josie's past being violent, but he kicked himself anyway. He should have guessed. Shouldn't have taken his frustrations out on the sweet ray of sunshine that kept trying to pierce his dark and gloomy moods. He didn't think he would ever get the image of her curled up on the floor in the fetal position out of his head.

God *damn,* he'd fucked up.

"Who the hell even *am* I anymore?"

He needed to talk to someone, but he didn't want to interrupt Roger and Jenna on their date. Fuck, he'd been a cranky asshole to them as well. And he should apologize to them, too. Josie definitely deserved more than just the apology he'd given her so far, but he already knew she wouldn't want to see him again tonight. He checked the time on his phone and sent Nadia a text.

Finn: Hey, you up?

Nadia: Not for much longer. Why?

Finn: I need ideas for how to apologize to a girl.

Nadia: It kinda depends on what you did. Did you spill her coffee or run over her dog? Are you romantically involved?

Finn: Let's say somewhere in the middle. And as for your second question, no.

Nadia: Flowers are generally a good apology. Just don't get her roses unless you want to date her.

Where the fuck was he going to find flowers when he couldn't drive?

> Finn: Pretty sure the only flowers Roger has growing around here are the dandelions.

> Nadia: DO NOT PICK HER DANDE-LIONS! YOU ARE NOT A CHILD!

> Finn: Okay, well, I'm just going to keep apologizing to her, I guess.

> Nadia: A wise woman once told me, "The best apology is changed behavior."

> Finn: That I can do. Thanks, sis.

> Nadia: You're welcome. Good night!

The next morning, he rose early for his appointment with Doctor Lopez. Roger had promised to take him, and Finn had gotten an idea while he tossed and turned last night to show Josie he was changing his behavior.

It started with looking at himself in the mirror, trying to remember who he'd been before the incident. Closing his eyes, he envisioned that version of himself in his mind. Taking deep breaths, he held onto that image while brushing his teeth and shaving the stubble off his chin. He dabbed his aftershave on his face, the first time he'd used it since he left the Marines.

He dressed himself in jeans and a t-shirt, but he took the stump sock downstairs in his hand. Roger, Jenna, and Josie were gathered around the island eating the scrambled eggs that Roger had cooked.

"Morning, Finn," his brother called out.

"Morning."

"Your plate's staying warm in the microwave."

"Thanks." Clearing his throat, Finn approached Josie, whose gray eyes darted to the side to watch him while she faced her plate. "Josie, could you help me with the shrinker?"

She blinked up at him, laying her fork down. "Sure." Her whispered reply didn't fool him. She was scared of him. And it was all his fault. Together, they pulled the stump shrinker up where it needed to go. He pulled his plate from the microwave and sat down on the empty bar stool next to Roger.

"Josie agreed to go with us to Bethesda, since she's going to be helping with your arm." Finn blinked in response. Hadn't she told him about what an asshole he'd been last night? Roger had no idea what he'd asked of her. He couldn't have, or he'd be telling Finn to pack his bag and go back to Mom and Dad's. Hell, why had she agreed to it? Why hadn't she run screaming?

Heart beating double-time in his chest, he lifted his head to stare at her in astonishment, just catching her gaze as it flitted back down to her plate. "Thank you." Her gaze lifted to his and caught him in a snare. She nodded, but looked away again.

Maybe he hadn't fucked up as badly as he thought? He scarfed down his breakfast, ready to get this appointment over with. And he took his pain pill just to make a point.

He'd done some searching on his phone last night, and apparently mood swings were a sign of chronic pain. Go figure.

Josie insisted on riding in the backseat, which Finn didn't agree with. Ladies should ride up front, but he let her choose where she was comfortable. Conversation was stilted, so Roger put on his classic rock radio station. While Whitesnake crooned *Is this Love,* Finn peeked back at Josie, only to see her leaning against the window, fast asleep. Guilt swamped him again, knowing she probably didn't get enough sleep because of his outburst setting her off. No more. He'd do better.

While on the way to Walter Reed, they stopped at a gas station. One of the big ones, with made to order food and a huge drink selection. Josie had to use the bathroom. Finn took advantage as well. Once he'd finished, he stood next to Roger, where he waited for Josie in the tiny hall.

"You look like a creeper, dude."

"You said bodyguard wrong."

"No, I didn't." But Finn just rolled his eyes. He had no idea why Josie needed protection, and after last night, he sure as hell wasn't going to pry.

After Josie exited the ladies' room, they all grabbed drinks from the cooler. After Roger had paid, they were exiting the building when Josie slammed against the wall.

"Roger... that guy next to the blue SUV."

Following her head tilt, Roger peeked outside and promptly ushered her back inside. "You recognize him?"

"Maybe? It's hard to say. But he looks like one of them."

Finn furrowed his brows. Surely no one would try anything with Roger right there?

Before he could say anything, he noticed the guy was getting into the vehicle. "Looks like he's leaving,"

"Let's wait for him to go."

Finn pulled out his phone and pretended to be checking something while he surreptitiously watched the guy out of the corner of his eye. "Pulling into traffic now."

"Okay. Stay between us, sweetheart."

Finn and Roger flanked Josie on the way to the truck, where she slid into the backseat and onto the floor. Once they were on the highway, she pulled herself up and he heard her seat belt click.

Weird. But he didn't feel like he had a right to ask questions. Roger had said if she wanted to tell him, she would. He had to wait for her.

Once they arrived at Walter Reed, Josie seemed like her normal self. She followed him into the doctor's office. He sat on the examination table, and Josie took the chair against the wall. An awkward silence descended.

But before he could think of what to say, Doctor Lopez knocked on the door.

"Good morning! How are you today?""Doin' alright."

She held her hand out to Josie. "Hi, I'm Doctor Lopez. Are you Finn's wife?"

Finn ignored how right that sounded as Josie turned bright red and stammered as she shook the doctor's hand.

"No, I'm just a... family friend, but I'm also a nurse. They asked me to help with his care. I'm Josie."

"Wonderful to meet you, Josie!" She turned back to Finn. "And you're okay discussing your care with Josie in the room?"

"Yes, ma'am."

"Wonderful. How's your pain today?" She pulled her tablet out from her long white coat and took out a stylus to take notes.

"Had to take a pill today." He still didn't like it.

"You don't sound happy about that."

"They make me woozy."

Doctor Lopez nodded. "Many patients feel that way. I can write you a script for something a bit weaker, but taken more frequently, it should work just fine. Then you can save the narcotics for a really bad day."

"Thanks, Doc." She listened to his heart and his lungs before motioning to him to remove his stump sock.

She gently palpated the amputation site as Finn turned his head. "How is the desensitization going?"

A lump formed in his throat as he thought of the disaster last night had been. But it was Josie that spoke first.

"He's still struggling with the rougher textures, but we're working on it."

Doctor Lopez hummed. "And the massage?"

"Working on it." Finn averted his eyes as he parroted Josie's phrase back to the doctor. He hated lying, even by omission. But he *was* going to work on it, so that counted, right?

She gave him a thoughtful look, then sat down on the wheeled stool. "How do you feel about the prosthesis?"

Finn shrugged.

"Do you want to put it off?"

"No!" He answered at once. "I want to try." Please, please let Josie see he was changing. That he would take care of himself.

"Alright. But don't overdo it. You're not required to wear one at all. It's for your comfort and your access, okay?"

"Yes, ma'am."

She demonstrated how to strap the arm on, advised him to take it off if the arm was irritated, and showed him how to lean forward with his shoulder to open and close the rubber hand. Grateful it didn't have a hook, and he wouldn't have to endure pirate jokes from now until the end of time, Finn played around. It had a limited range of motion, and it would take time to get used to the weirdness of using his shoulder to control it. But it would do.

Standing in front of the mirrored elevator doors, he frowned at the reflection staring back at him. Roger behind him. Josie next to him, both perfect and whole, and he had what looked like a doll's arm on his right side. Why was he even worried about his looks? He'd already decided he'd be a permanent bachelor.

When the elevator opened and let them inside, Roger noticed his mood shift. "Something on your mind?"

Finn just shook his head, already feeling the spiral sucking him into the whirlpool of self-doubt and bad moods. Bad moods he was supposed to be doing better at, damn it. Why had he pushed to start using the arm?

Walking outside the hospital, they passed through a green space that butted up next to a busy road on the way to the truck. Finn had sunk deep into thought, his memories rising up, when a car backfired.

But it didn't sound like a car backfiring to him. The Maryland landscape fell away and turned into the desert. His unit patrolled through a village, and a shot rang out.

"Get down!" He turned and threw Vasquez to the ground, rolling them behind a wall to be safe from the bullets he knew would rain down any second.

"Finn?" He blinked. That didn't sound like Vasquez. And since when did she call him anything other than Hunt?

Was something wrong with her voice?

"Finn, it's okay." Cold hands cupped his face, which didn't make sense. It was a hundred degrees outside...

"It was just a car, Finn." Josie lay beneath him on the ground, a juniper bush hiding them from the street. Her thumbs stroked his cheeks as he came back to reality. Walter Reed. Bethesda.

"Shit! I'm sorry, Josie." Finn pushed himself to his knees with his left hand. His stomach sank. She could have been hurt, and he wouldn't have had any idea.

"You could at least buy her dinner first." Roger, that jackass, slapped him on the shoulder and helped them both up.

Then, the most amazing thing happened. Josie tipped her head back and *laughed*. The music she made erased his embarrassment, and he started to chuckle along. He'd make a fool of himself every day just to hear that sound.

When they got back to the truck, she got into the back again and Roger dropped his voice while they were alone. "Seriously, Bro, you okay?"

"I uh, I am now."

"You should probably talk to someone." As if he knew Finn was about to argue, he continued. "What if you'd been on concrete?"

Finn squeezed his eyes shut. "I'll do a search tonight."

"I'm here for you, too."

"And I owe you an apology for being a cranky asshole."

"I served, too. I get it. We're good."

"Thanks." They embraced quickly and hopped into the truck to go home.

As they drove back toward Baltimore, Finn got an idea. Turning in his seat, he looked back at her. "I guess I owe you dinner."

Josie stammered. Roger shook his head. "It'd be dinner for three, Finn. Jenna or I need to go with her for protection."

"Well, I'm not totally useless in the kitchen. Can I make you dinner?"

"Um, when?"

He'd need time to get groceries. And to figure out something simple that he could do with one hand. "Tomorrow?" He held his breath, watching her for an answer.

She gnawed on her lip, but finally she answered. "Okay."

His grin spread across his face for the first time since he'd woken up in that hospital in Germany. "How's six?"

"Sure."

When they pulled up to the house, Mom and Jon were standing on Roger's porch. His pulse pounded in his ears. He owed Mom an apology, too.

"Finn! The arm looks great."

"Thanks, Mom. It feels like I'm mutating into an action figure." He stepped up to the porch, holding out his arms. "But at least I can do this." Then he wrapped her up in a hug. The first real hug *should* belong to his mom. She took her time hugging him back, which he deserved. "I'm sorry that I've been such a grumpy bastard."

"If you need anything…" Her voice wobbled with tears.

"Can you take me to the grocery store tomorrow afternoon?"

She pulled back. "The grocery store?"

He nodded. "I need ingredients."

"Sure! Sure. I'll pick you up at one?"

"Perfect. Thanks, Mom." He turned to Jon. "What are you doing here?"

"Can't I come see my family?" Jon teased him right back.

"Come on in," Roger said as he unlocked the door. "What brings you by?"

"Well, you didn't answer your phone, and neither did Finn." Jon pulled his jacket off and hung it on a hook by the front door. "So Mom called me. She wanted to know how Finn's appointment went."

Roger shrugged. "I was driving."

Finn pulled his phone out and saw a missed call from his mom. "I had it on silent while we were in the appointment and just forgot to turn it back up."

"We?" Mom looked confused, and Finn felt the blood drain out of his face. How could he explain Josie's presence at his doctor's appointment without his mother thinking they were dating?

Mom had been on her boys to settle down for years, although Finn always had a ready excuse with the Marines. Now, he didn't, and it had just occurred to him she'd try to set him up as soon as possible.

Roger to the rescue. "Josie's got a nursing degree, so she's going to help Finn with his home care."

"Oh, right. I forgot Roger told me you're a nurse. That makes sense."

"Well, not exactly. I haven't sat for my boards yet, so I don't have the license, but I have the degree. And I really appreciate Finn giving me the chance to practice a little so I can walk into a job interview with some experience."

Finn breathed a silent sigh of relief. *Nice save, Josie.*

"That's wonderful. I feel so much better knowing you have a professional in the house." She patted his arm. "Well, I'll see you tomorrow. Glad the arm is working out."

"Bye, Mom."

Roger locked the door behind her, and turned to Jon. "So, what did you want to talk about?"

"I have an idea for a campaign, and I want you guys to be in it, just like old times."

Chapter 14

"Campaign?" Josie asked.

"*Dungeons and Dragons.*" Roger said with a grin. "I guess you were bound to find out our horrible secret eventually." She gulped. Her memories supplied one of her father's tirades, going on about the satanic nature of a game where people hunted dragons and killed for treasure. In all honesty, she tended to tune him out when he ranted like that. Could it be the same thing? "What's that?"

"We're giant nerds." Jon's straight white teeth gleamed at her as he chuckled. "Not only do we play *D&D*, we LARP, too."

"Man," Finn groaned. "I can't LARP anymore. How can I hold a sword with Ken over here?" He waved his prosthetic arm around with jerky movements.

Nerds? They were the furthest thing from the buck-toothed caricature that word conjured. "What's LARP?"

"It stands for Live Action Role Play. Which makes us the nerdiest of the nerds in the hierarchy. Basically, we get together and beat another team of nerds with foam weapons and act out damage as if we got wounded." At her wide-eyed stare, Roger continued. "There're rules and stuff. It's very civilized."

She blinked, trying not to imagine these three buff men as warriors.

"It's how I met Jenna, actually. She was just there as a trial run. She didn't like the game that much. But that's originally how we met."

"Dude." Finn punched him in the arm. "You didn't tell me that."

"Imagine my surprise when I show up to her apartment and find out *she's* who I'm supposed to guard." Roger shook his head. "Weird way to run into a one-night stand."

Jon and Finn laughed and ribbed him some more, but Roger took it good-naturedly.

"So we going to play at your place or mine?"

"If we can stick to weekends, let's play here. You've got all the books, anyway."

Roger rubbed his chin. "Do you need to borrow some to work on the campaign?"

"Yes, please."

"How do you play it?" She couldn't help but ask.

Roger wandered over to the bookshelf in the living room and pulled out a couple of well-worn hardcover books with elaborate illustrations on the cover. "Finn, do you want to explain it to her while Jon and I go over dungeon master stuff?"

"Sure." He took one of the books and ushered Josie over to the island. "Where are your dice?"

His brother tossed him a small fabric bag, which Finn caught in both hands. Both hands. He stared down in wonder and gave an incredulous laugh. "Holy shit. I didn't even think about it." Josie's breath caught in her throat at the beatific grin that took over his face.

All the Hunt brothers were good-looking, but in her opinion, Finn was the most handsome.

Roger and Jon went into his office and Josie slid onto one of the bar stools at the kitchen island. Finn sat down next to her, laying the book on the counter with the dice.

"These are Roger's dice. We can get you your own set, or I have a spare set at my parents' house you can use, if you want."

The dice Finn poured out of the bag were all different shapes. One was the usual cube, but one was a pyramid, and one looked like two pyramids glued together. And the other two were shapes she'd never seen before.

Finn lined them up in a row, starting with the pyramid and the cube, and ending with the two really weird ones. "Each of these has a different number of sides." He picked up the cube and showed it to her. "You're probably used to a six-sided die, right?"

"Yes."

"This one has four sides." He pointed to the pyramid and worked his way down the line. "Eight. Ten. And this is a twenty-sided die." He handed her the one at the end. It really did have numbers one through twenty inscribed on it.

"Did you have a Magic Eight ball when you were a kid?"

Josie shook her head emphatically no. "My parents would never have allowed it. It was too close to witch-craft."

Finn smirked. "It's actually just a twenty-sided die with words instead of numbers, floating around in a big ball." He turned the twenty right side up. "It is certain." Then he flipped it to the one. "My reply is no." He laid it back down on the counter. "I forget the rest of them, but you get the idea."

Josie sat there, stunned. Then she started to laugh. "You mean my parents were afraid of a toy, with nothing but a *die inside*?" It was so ridiculous that she couldn't stop laughing, and Finn chuckled along even as he reached over and patted her on the back when she hiccupped and gasped for air. What other completely harmless things had her parents feared?

When she got her breathing under control, she wiped tears from her eyes and looked up at him. "I'm okay. Please, continue."

"We use these to determine outcomes of just about everything in the game. Each one is referred to by their number. So this one is a D20." He pointed down the line. "D10, D8, D6, and D4." He opened up the book and showed her some of the rules. "So when your character hits another with a sword, the victim takes two D4 damage. That means he rolls two D4s, or rolls one of them twice, and adds the numbers together, to find out how many hit points he lost."

"Hit points?"

"Your health, basically. We call them hit points because that's how many hits you can take. Get it?" She nodded.

Finn flipped back to the beginning of the book, and she found herself leaning closer, reading over the different races and classes she could play. As Finn talked about each one's traits and special abilities, his face animated.

"How did you—" She turned her head and found Finn's face much closer than she'd anticipated, close enough to watch his pupils dilate in his pale green eyes. His breaths fanned her cheek, and her gaze dropped to his lips. Fluttering in her chest distracted her from what she wanted to ask.

"How did I what?" he asked in a soft voice, as though afraid to break the spell.

"Um..." She licked her lips as she tried to think. It was only because she was sitting so close that she heard his whispered groan, and then he pulled slightly back, releasing her.

"How did I do what, Sunshine?"

Finn's normal tone broke the enchantment, and Josie gave herself a subtle shake. "How did you get into... this?" She waved her hand at the book and dice on the counter.

He smiled, but it didn't reach his eyes. Was he... disappointed? "My big brothers, of course. There weren't a lot of games that we could all play together, since we're so far apart in age."

"Really?" She hadn't noticed.

"Roger's ten years older than me. Jon was six when I was born. And Nadia didn't come along until six years after that. A teenager doesn't want to play Candy Land all the time, even if it is for his youngest brother."

Josie wondered idly if Judy had any pictures of the boys playing games that she could peek at. Finn would have been an adorable kid.

"They could tailor the game to whoever was playing. And when Roger joined the Army, we kept it going long distance. Even when Jon was at the Naval Academy. It gave us a way to stay connected even when we were spread around the country."

"That's beautiful." Josie rubbed at the ache in her chest when she thought about her six siblings stuck back in Montana with her parents. Would Jocelyn be graduating from high school yet? Had Jeb gotten to go to college? Walking away from them had been the hardest thing about leaving, but she'd thought Brad was her future.

"Anyway," Finn cleared his throat. "If you want to play with us, you're more than welcome. I'll help you roll up a character. It's a little daunting the first time."

And that's how they passed the time, heads together pouring over the player handbook.

WHEN MOM PICKED HIM up the following afternoon, she was driving his truck.

"Mom! You hate driving my truck." Finn walked up to where she idled in the driveway, his mouth open in awe.

She squared her shoulders and lifted her chin. "That doesn't mean I can't."

He looked over his F-150 with fondness. He'd missed the old girl. His occupational therapist had explained he would have to prove he was safe to drive before he could get behind the wheel again, and had given him a list of places he could take the truck to discuss adaptations he could have done, but no one had availability until after the new year.

"Hey, Mom, what's an easy dinner I can make essentially one-handed?"

Mom shrugged. "Spaghetti? You might need help with the jar of sauce, though."

"No, that's perfect. I can always get Roger to open it if it's too hard."

"What brought this on?"

Oh shit. If he told her what he was really doing, she'd smell blood in the water, and he'd never convince her he wasn't dating Josie. "I wanted to make dinner for everyone, since Roger's letting me stay there."

"That's lovely, dear."

But was jarred sauce enough? Surely he could make it from scratch. Or at least, cans, right?

He didn't have time to boil and skin fresh tomatoes.

When they arrived at the grocery store, Mom grabbed a cart.

"What did you need?"

Finn took his own cart. "I kinda wanted to shop by myself." God, he was a grown man, and Mom was nowhere near ready for the retirement home.

"But I thought we could spend time together!"

He braced himself. The last thing he needed her questioning was why he was only making dinner for two. Plus, he'd been around people nonstop for months. Even holing himself up in his room hadn't worked. He needed to feel like an independent person again.

"Mom, it's the grocery store, not board game night." He winced as she huffed in disappointment. "I'll meet you at the front when I'm done, okay?"

"Alright."

She turned and walked away. Finn blew out a breath, trying to ignore the gnawing feeling that his arm would draw stares.

But it didn't. He pulled up a simple recipe for marinara sauce on his phone, bookmarked it, and headed for the pasta aisle.

While he was searching for some ground beef to add to the sauce, someone tapped him on the shoulder. "Finn?"

Turning, Finn's jaw dropped when he spied his old rifle coach, Curt Atkins. After fifteen-plus years, he'd put on some weight, and his hair was completely gray now, but Finn would know him anywhere. He was even still wearing the same hat with the name of the high school on it. "Hey, Coach." When Coach reached out to shake his hand, his frown returned. "Uh, hang on." He placed the package of beef down in his cart and then stuck out his left hand to shake. It took Coach a minute to realize why.

"My God, Finn. What happened?"

There was no pity in his eyes like Finn had feared, only concern, but a lump formed in Finn's throat, anyway. "Roadside bomb in the Middle East."

"That was you? On the news last month?"

Finn shrugged. He didn't know what the news outlets were told or how much they told the public. "Might be. I was a bit busy."

"Are you home for good?"

"Yeah. Not much use for a sniper with one arm. And the blast damaged my eyesight." One corner of his mouth lifted at the irony. "I'm no Eagle Eye anymore."

Coach crossed his arms over his winter coat. "You had a good career, Finn. I'm sorry it ended like this."

Finn shrugged. What else could he do?

"What are you doing these days?"

Dropping his gaze, he shook his head. "Staying with my brother and trying not to drive everyone crazy."

"Would you have time to talk to the team?"

Finn's head shot up. He'd gotten taller than Coach Atkins in the years since he'd graduated, so it was weird looking down at the man. "The team?"

"Yeah, I got a few years of coachin' left in me, so I'm still at the high school. I talk about you every year when the kids wonder what they're going to do with their experience. Would you come talk to them at practice sometime?"

Finn's eyebrow rose. If Coach wanted him there, he'd be there. "You guys still practice at the same range?"

"Yep. Tuesdays and Thursdays, four to six."

They exchanged phone numbers, and Finn relished the idea of talking to the kids about his experience in the Marines. The good parts, anyway. He could do that and avoid talking about the friends he'd lost.

Chapter 15

Josie was sitting on the couch going over her notes for the NCLEX when a truck approached the house. Finn strode in through the front door, bags in his left hand.

"Do you want some help?"

"I got it." He flashed a smile at her, and Josie swallowed against the lump in her throat. That thing was lethal.

"I hope you like pasta."

"I love it."

She curled back up on the couch to read while Finn rustled about in the kitchen. At some point, Roger exited his office and headed for the stairs, but he stopped off at the couch first.

"Jenna and I are going to hang out upstairs, but if you need us, just holler, okay?" She nodded. Roger smirked. "I think you're good for my brother in more than one way."

Her cheeks heated, but she played dumb. "I don't know what you mean."

"Keep telling yourself that." He chuckled and went upstairs to do whatever he and Jenna were going to do. She'd heard a television up there before, so maybe they would watch a movie.

Tired of reading the same stuff over and over, Josie wandered into the kitchen and leaned against the island. Finn was stirring ground beef into the tomato sauce while the pasta boiled.

"Can I do anything?"

Finn spun around. There were tiny splatters of red on his gray Henley, and he had a spoon in his hand. "You can sit and keep me company, if you want." He laid the spoon down, then reached into the cabinet above and grabbed two plates and two bowls. A timer buzzed, and he slid on an oven mitt to pull golden brown, buttery garlic bread out of the oven. Her stomach growled. "The noodles are almost done, so I just have to pour the salad. I got bagged salad mix. I hope that's okay."

Goodness. He'd gone all out. And with one hand, too. "It's great. I'm honored, really."

"I'm no chef, but I should learn how to cook more things, now that there's no mess hall to rely on."

They sat down to possibly the first meal she'd ever had a man cook for her that wasn't on the grill. He'd even served something green when she'd had to fight Brad to even *buy* vegetables. And the fact that he'd cooked for *just* her made her feel special.

But he was her patient, and she was on a …. what had Jenna called it? A man ban. Not that Jenna knew she was on one. She'd been explaining how she hadn't been looking for romance when she met Roger, and that she hadn't wanted to get close to anyone.

Finn would be at the top of Josie's list when her ban ended, though.

He hesitated when it came to drinks. "I got wine, but I wasn't sure if you drank. And I'm not supposed to drink with my pain medicine."

"Water is fine. I don't really drink."

"Sounds good." He poured them each a glass from the filtration pitcher in the refrigerator and sat across from her.

If you ignored the fact they were in his brother's kitchen, it almost felt like a date.

"Are you from around here?"

Josie shook her head as she poured the dressing over her salad and speared some on her fork. "I'm from Montana, actually."

"Really? How do you like it here?"

"I haven't spent much time out about town, but I like it so far." It was certainly better than going back to her parents.

His brow wrinkled at that. "How long will it be before you can move about freely?"

"I don't know." She put her fork down, biting her lip.

He reached across the island toward her. "I'm sorry. I didn't mean to make you uncomfortable. Of course, you don't want to talk about it."

She took his hand, but she wanted to tell him *some*thing. Not everything, not yet. "We have to wait for the FBI to investigate and do their thing. The people that brought me to Baltimore don't know where I am, and we want it to stay that way."

His jaw set, and his eyes blazed with an intense fire as his hand gripped hers. But he didn't say anything else. He didn't have to.

After a moment of squeezing her hand that didn't go on long enough, he withdrew, and she reluctantly went back to eating.

"Tell me about some of the *Dungeons and Dragons'* games you played as kids. What was the funniest ... time?"

He told her about the session where Jon's character had gotten himself beat up when he flirted with the captain of the guard's wife in a town they'd been passing through. About that time Nadia joined, and they were attacked by an army, so her sorcerer cast "Magic Mansion" ten feet above the army's heads, and crushed them. Roger had thrown up his hands in defeat and they'd had to end the session early.

They were laughing and joking, filling up on spaghetti and garlic bread. At some point the doorbell rang, but Roger jogged down the steps to get it, toss his money at the delivery guy and disappear back upstairs with a bag of food.

This was, for all intents and purposes, a date. And Josie didn't know what to think about that. Instead of over-thinking it, she enjoyed herself. Why shouldn't she? The grumpy man she'd first encountered in this house had come out of his shell. Plus, it wasn't every day she had a hot military man cooking *her* dinner.

Maybe if she hadn't jumped at the first man to pay her any sort of attention, she wouldn't be in this position. But then she wouldn't have left her parents' strict house and church, and she wouldn't be here right now.

"Why the Marines?" she found herself asking.

Finn twirled the few remaining noodles around on his fork, thinking. "I wanted to be different from my brothers," he finally admitted. "Roger decided after 9/11 that he wanted to go into the Army. Dropped out of college after one semester. A few years later, Jon decided to be different and join the Navy. So when the Marine recruiter approached me senior year after the state rifle competition, I figured I would do something different."

"The few, the proud?"

Finn smirked. "We all do different jobs, and we might give each other hell, but we're all on the same side."

"Why not the Air Force?"

"Well, they don't really have snipers in the Air Force. And that's how the recruiter got my attention."

"Sounds more like you got his attention. You must have done well."

A small smile graced his lips. "I won."

Josie's eyes about popped out of her head. "No wonder they wanted you."

A pink tinge colored his cheeks, making him even more adorable. "My dress uniform has a lot of medals on it."

It should bother her, shouldn't it? That he was capable of such violence. But Josie felt nothing but secure with him. This man wouldn't hurt anyone that didn't deserve it. And since that one night where he sent her into a panic attack, he hadn't so much as raised his voice. Somehow, she knew, he was making progress.

Now that everyone was within driving distance, Mom had declared Sunday night to be family dinner night. Roger offered to drive all four of them, since his truck had the extended cab. Which meant Finn rode next to Josie and needed a distraction.

"Ooh, Chevy is so fancy with their extended cab. Next thing you know, they'll build an electric truck." He teased Roger. "You know Ford makes an extended cab, too, right? If you want to stick with Fix Or Repair Daily."

"Hey! I haven't had any trouble with that truck."

"Because you're never home to drive it!" Roger laughed and Finn crossed his arms over his chest, frowning at him in the rearview mirror. "It's barely got any miles on it."

"Which means it will last even longer."

"Do you guys have this argument often?" Josie leaned over and whispered to him.

Taking in her worried expression, Finn patted her hand to put her at ease. God, her skin was so soft. "It's just good-natured teasing between the three of us. We all drove the Chevy Prism, the car Nadia drives now, but that's because it was Roger's first. Us guys all picked different branches of the military and we have different makes of pickup truck. We tease each other about both all the time."

She sat back with a nod, sliding her hand slowly away. Finn left his on the seat between them, an ache starting to bloom in his chest. Everything had gone so well last night.

And why was he worried about her rejecting him? She deserved someone whole. But when she'd pulled away from him that night after he lost his shit, he'd realized he didn't want her to be afraid of him. She'd clearly had cause to fear someone else in her life. At the very least, he could be her protector until someone worthy came along.

And he'd be ... nope. Not going to think about it.

They pulled into the house next to Nadia's Prism and Jon's flashy red Dodge Ram. Before Josie could open her door, Finn laid a hand on her shoulder. "I'll come around for you," he whispered into her ear. Her cheeks turned pink, but she nodded.

His breath made clouds in the chilly evening air. While Roger rounded the front of the truck to get Jenna's door, Finn went around the back. Someone, probably a man, hadn't treated Josie right, and he was determined to show her how she should be treated. Even if she couldn't be his. He could give her that much.

Holding out his good hand to help her down, Finn marveled at the idea that anyone would treat Josie as less than a princess. If he ever met the guy that had raised a hand to her, he'd rip off his arm and beat him with it.

At least it'd be useful for something.

Roger called out as he opened their parents' front door. Voices echoed from the dining room. He let Josie go ahead of him, but he regretted it the minute he realized Roger and Jenna had sat across from Jon, and the only seats available were with him.

"Josie, come sit by me," his squid brother said, his grin wide. "I don't bite. Unless you ask nicely."

Finn growled as he glared down at the brother with a death wish.

"Finn!" Nadia chastised him. "Knock it off." Her green eyes darted to his right, where Josie shied away from him. Crap, he was upsetting her.

Swallowing his groan, he slid the middle chair next to Jon out and sank his ass into it, leaving Josie the one on the end next to his mother.

"Seriously, Jon, you need to stop flirting with my clients." Thank God Roger was taking over the glaring. Meanwhile, Finn found Jenna glaring his way. The look on the feisty redhead's face said she wasn't happy with his caveman behavior.

Nadia pulled her glasses down to scold him. "This is why I call you three Neanderthals."

Jon's laugh carried a nervous edge to it. "It's all in good fun, right, Josie?"

Finn glanced over at the silent woman next to him. Her gaze was glued to her empty plate. Damn it, he'd fucked up again. *And* his brother was an asshole. Leaning over so only she could hear him, he murmured an apology.

"I'm sorry." He didn't know why Jon's advance had made her nervous, but he knew he shouldn't have responded that way.

Her gray eyes took in his face, and she gave him a subtle nod.

Mom sat down and slipped her napkin into her lap. "I'm sorry for my sons' idiotic behavior. I promise they mean well." When Josie nodded at Mom, she continued. "Let's forget it and say grace."

Dinner went by uneventfully if you didn't count Mom harassing Nadia and Caleb for the wedding details. Now that he was no longer Mom's concern, Finn guessed she'd moved on to her other pet project. And since he wasn't going anywhere anytime soon, they could finally pick a date.

Not that Mom was happy with the date. She wanted Nadia to get married in June.

"We can't get a venue that quickly, Mom. I want a fall wedding, anyway."

After dinner, it was a relief to take the dishes out to the kitchen. Josie brought out more dishes, and they teamed up at the sink, her rinsing and him placing the dirty dishes into the dishwasher.

"Hey, Finn, look up!"

He turned his head backward to see Roger giving him a sneaky grin. "Why?"

"Just do it!" His oldest brother called out, distracting everyone at the table and making them turn to look at him and Josie.

"Uh, oh..." Josie's quiet sound made him look up as well. A green and white bundle hung off the wooden trim over the kitchen sink. He looked back down at Josie to see her cheeks red and her teeth sinking into her lower lip.

His heart beat against his chest. "We don't have to if you don't want to," he offered. This wasn't how he would have wanted this to happen.

Her eyes darted back and forth as she considered his offer.

Now it was Nadia's turn to interfere. "It's bad luck if you don't!"

Josie's teeth sank into her lush bottom lip. "I think I've had all the bad luck I can stand this year."

"Alright."

She screwed her eyes shut, and Finn leaned down to press his lips against hers in a chaste kiss that left his lips tingling.

A moment, and then it was over.

"Boo!" cried Jon from the dining room. "Kiss her for real!"

Finn rolled his eyes, but he wrapped his left arm around her shoulders and pulled her back to him, at the same time lifting his middle finger to Jon, who howled.

He could give her a real kiss. He'd give her everything if she'd let him.

Chapter 16

JOSIE'S HANDS FLATTENED AGAINST Finn's pectorals as his lips descended on hers again. The first one had left her desperate for more, but now electricity flowed through her like Finn's mouth was a battery. His tongue slid along the line of her lips, requesting entry, and she tentatively opened for him. Then she was surrounded, filled, and overcome with heat. Her fingers clenched his Henley. Closer, closer, she wanted to be closer still. She could crawl inside this man and still not be close enough.

Wolf whistles broke through her haze and Finn pulled away, his mouth red and his chest heaving under her fingertips. That's when she registered not only the bulge in his jeans but also the moisture between her legs. Holy crap. She hadn't ruined a pair of panties since she'd cut off her family, back when things with Brad were still good. After her time in captivity, Josie had wondered if she'd ever feel desire again.

Well, now she had her answer.

And in front of his *family*, too.

"I'll be back," she murmured, pulling out of his embrace, and dashed for the bathroom.

Shutting the door behind her, Josie leaned back against the wood and watched herself in the mirror as her breathing slowed. Her cheeks flamed and her eyes sparkled, and she almost didn't recognize herself.

She ran cool water over her wrists, trying to cool herself off at her pulse points. Then she splashed the cold water on her face and used the toilet, so no one would know how embarrassed she was. Finn was a far better kisser than her ex. She didn't remember a man turning her on like *that* before. Her heart still raced, and she ran cold water over her pulse again, wondering if she could ask Jenna for some ChapStick. Her mouth still tingled.

A knock on the door disrupted her reverie. Crap, she'd been in here too long. Finn's voice came through the door on something close to a whisper. "You okay? I'm sorry, I'm sure that was... a lot."

Oh gosh. Finn thought she was upset? "You didn't hurt me. I was just surprised. And now I'm really embarrassed because... you're my patient." She couldn't say the real reason. Admitting she needed new panties was too personal when she had never talked about sex with anyone who wasn't her ex. She wasn't even sure what she liked in the bedroom. He'd never asked.

Finn was silent on the other side of the door long enough for her to compose herself. "You sure you're okay?"

Josie opened the door and nearly startled as Finn was there, taking up the entire door. He looked down into her eyes, and she hoped he could see everything she couldn't say.

Josie's cheeks flamed once more as she stammered. Finn gave her a soft smile and took her hand. "Come on. Let's show them you're alright. I think Mom is still scolding Nadia and Jon."

With a snort, Josie followed him back to the dining room, taking their seats once more. She turned to face him, to say something, but she wasn't sure what. And the intense look he gave her took her breath away. He searched her face, worry carved into his expression.

He really was such a good guy. She reached out and rested her hand on her shoulder. "We're good," she murmured. The tension seeped out of his body, and he relaxed into his chair.

The rest of the evening passed without incident. No one mentioned their mistletoe kiss, even after arriving back at Roger and Jenna's house. But every time she looked at him, she found herself looking at his mouth and remembering.

Finn came around to get her door again, an unnecessary but touching gesture that warmed her chest. The temperature had dropped now that night had fallen. Thankful for the winter coat Roger's family had sourced from somewhere, a part of her missed the Montana winters. The Rockies always looked so pretty covered in snow. But Baltimore was starting to feel like home.

She did some more studying until the shower turned off, then replaced her bookmark and hopped up to take her turn. As she moved to shut the door to Finn's room, grunting caught her attention.

Josie slowly opened the door once more. Finn sat on his bed, pain scrunching his face. His left hand cupped his right stump, where he attempted to manipulate it the way the doctor had explained it. But he was pushing himself way too hard.

"Do you want some help?" flew from her lips before she thought better of it. At least she was far enough away if she upset him again.

He dropped his hand and looked up. "Please," he sighed. "I can't bring myself to do it, and when I do, I'm so tense I just want to get it over with—"

"And that's not helpful in your situation." She walked forward, grateful she hadn't stripped for the shower yet. Finn's incredible chest was on display, all smooth, tanned skin. When she got closer, she realized he was only wearing his boxer briefs. She might have only recently rediscovered her libido, but she could be professional about this.

He slid down the bed to let her sit on his right side, and she gave his amputation site a good look for the first time. "Lift for me." He rotated his shoulder and lifted his stump in front of him. It was angry and red. "This looks painful. You should take off the prosthesis when it gets uncomfortable."

Finn dropped his chin. "I know, but I like wearing it. It's not much, but it's *some*thing, you know?" She gently prodded at it with her fingertips while he paused. "I don't feel so broken with it."

"You're not broken." He lifted his head and raised one eyebrow at her. "You have a limb difference. That's all."

He snorted but said nothing. Josie set about calming the nerves in his arm with the Lamaze techniques she'd learned while studying labor and delivery. But they helped with all kinds of pain. Finn shuddered.

"Wow, that feels… good." His surprise bled into his tone.

Josie just smiled and set about lightly massaging the flesh at the end of his arm in light circles with one hand, while distracting him by stroking along the bicep. Then she realized he'd forgotten a crucial step.

"Did you put on the moisturizing cream like the doctor talked about?"

"No. Why would I need to moisturize it?"

"Because it softens the scar and will keep the skin more pliant." She reached for the plastic bag the doctor had sent home with him. It was sitting on the floor next to the nightstand. She opened the tiny sample tube and put a dollop on her finger. Finn looked at her skeptically. "Trust me? It will make this easier."

He shrugged. "Okay."

She rubbed the cream back and forth, up and down, and as the skin started to absorb it, she used her thumb to massage it in a circular motion. Finn groaned. His head was thrown back, his eyes closed. "Am I hurting you?"

"No," he croaked. His left hand shifted, and he muttered something that sounded like, "Get back in your seat."

"Pardon?"

"Not you." His voice strained.

"Finn, what's wrong?"

"Let's just say that feels too good, and I'm dealing with a situation here." His cheeks turned red, and that's when the penny fell.

"Oh." Her gaze dropped to his lap against her better judgment, where his hand cupped over his crotch.

"I'm sorry."

"Don't be. I'm a big boy and I can deal with it."

"I just... I thought... after that kiss..."

Finn shook his head with vehemence. "You have no obligation or anything like that. I wouldn't push you for something you weren't willing to give." Then he grimaced. "Except I totally pushed it with that kiss. I let Jon get into my head. I'm so sorry."

"No, Finn, I—I liked it." She bit her lip and looked away. "To be honest, I thought my libido was dead. Until tonight."

"What do you mean?"

Shoot. She hadn't meant to tell him about this tonight. Looking back at him, his sharp eyes were taking her in.

"I—I don't like talking about it." Her voice trembled, and she hated it. "But let's just say I didn't get any choices until I met your brother and Jenna."

The silence hung in the air between them, laced with meaning she didn't want him to grasp. Not yet. Finally, he nodded.

"I'm here if you want to talk. Or not talk. Consider this me volunteering as tribute for you to explore to your heart's content."

She bristled. "I'm not a virgin."

"I didn't think you were," he answered, his voice soft. "But that doesn't mean you've had pleasure, and you deserve it. You deserve all the pleasure and I'm happy to let you figure out what you like without expecting anything in return."

"You mean, you would let me please myself, but you wouldn't... orgasm?" She whispered the last word, still scandalous in her mind, her brows furrowed, and her head tilted in confusion.

"I can't guarantee I could hold it off, Sunshine." His lips twitched in the start of a smile. "But that wouldn't be my goal."

"That doesn't seem fair to you!"

He shrugged. "My left hand is just as good as my right was. I can take care of business when you're satisfied." Her pulse beat in her ears. "In case you haven't figured it out, I'm wildly attracted to you, Josie."

She pushed her hair behind her ears. "I've only had one boyfriend." And a bunch of experience she didn't want, but she wasn't sure that counted.

"My only long-term relationship has been with the Marines. Any girls I've been with before knew that."

She nodded. "I'm attracted to you, too." And this wouldn't get in the way of her plans, would it? No, in fact, it would be perfect. But still, she shouldn't rush into anything. What if she freaked out again?

"But what's in it for you?"

Finn shrugged. God, him sitting there shirtless made it nearly impossible to think. "There's not much in this nurse job for you, is there?"

"Roger promised to write me a referral."

"But he's not paying you."

Josie frowned. "I should be paying him for letting me stay here, even if it has to wait until this whole thing is over. But he won't hear of it. This is the least I can do."

"You could consider it a trade." Finn was annoyingly calm, yet insistent. "Lessons in pleasure for taking care of my sorry ass."

Josie had to smother a laugh. He was really set on doing this. And desensitizing herself to men sounded like an excellent idea. Especially after that kiss.

She prayed she wasn't blushing as she answered. "I appreciate the offer. I'll think about it." And talk to her therapist.

He nodded. "Take your time." He glanced down at his arm. "Thanks for the help."

Sitting next to him on this bed, now that she wasn't actively massaging his stump, Josie suddenly registered how close they were. Finn leaned forward, but all he kissed was her cheek. "Good night, Josie."

"Good night." Rising from the bed, she headed back to the bathroom, praying he couldn't see the tight peaks of her nipples through her bra and shirt. She felt his lips against her cheek long after the door had shut.

SOMETIME IN THE MIDDLE of the night, Finn woke from a dead sleep. His heart pounded like the time his base had been attacked on his second deployment. What the hell? Just as he was about to roll back over, he heard a woman crying out. Josie?

Before he registered what he was doing, he'd opened the bathroom door, where it sounded like the yelling was. But it *was* Josie. Her screams about ripped his chest apart.

"No! *No!*"

He flipped the light on in the bathroom and ripped the door to her room open, prepared to face an intruder and holler for Roger. But no one stood next to her bed in the light spilling over. The window was shut tight.

Josie thrashed about in her sheets, wrapped up like a cocoon. Tears streamed down her face, her limbs fighting to get free.

"Josie! Josie! It's okay, you're dreaming." He bent over the bed and placed his hand on her shoulder, but that only made her scream louder.

"*No, no, no!*"

Finn panted as he started to panic. How to wake her, how to wake her? Finally, he ran for the light switch in desperation, flooding the room with light.

Gasping, her eyes started to blink open.

"That's it," he crooned, barely holding onto his calm. "Wake up, Sunshine."

As his voice registered, she opened her eyes the rest of the way. Glancing down at herself, she struggled against the sheet again, but less frantic this time.

"Can I help you out of there?" At her nod, Finn pulled the sheet out from around her, loosening it until she could get herself free. Fresh tears flowed, and she wrapped her arms around herself and shook.

He sat next to her on the bed and wiped her tears away. "You're okay. It was just a nightmare." The next thing he knew, he had an armful of crying woman. His chest warmed, and he wrapped her up in what passed for his embrace, just grateful she trusted him. "Let it out, baby. You're safe with me. Just let it all out." He rubbed his hand up and down her back, gently rocking her as she released the nightmare.

After she'd cried herself out, he went to get up, but she latched onto him. "Please don't leave."

"I'll stay. I was just going to get the light." When she nodded, he rose and quickly slapped the light switch off, leaving the small lamp on the nightstand on. "Better?"

She nodded again and lifted the covers. Her pajama shirt was askew, and he couldn't help but notice most of her perky breast peeking out. No nipple, but this was not the time.

Whatever had happened was bad, and he had to let her come to him.

He slid under the covers and let her crawl back into his embrace. Exhausted, her breathing evened out almost immediately.

Breathing a sigh of relief, Finn closed his eyes and memorized everything about holding her. Her warmth, her weight, her little snuffled breaths. All the tension leeched out of his body, and he relaxed fully into the mattress. He'd missed the feeling of being needed.

Chapter 17

Josie's pillow was warm and firm as she drifted back to consciousness. Morning sun streamed in golden beams through the split in the curtains, forcing her eyes open. She felt like a wrung-out washcloth, but somehow still rested. When her eyes blinked open, she realized her pillow wasn't a pillow at all. It was Finn! When did he get there?

And he was still asleep.

He looked so young as he lay there with his face relaxed. Her eyes wandered further south, looking at the impressive torso she'd had to ignore last night. Oh, how she wanted to let her hand drift down over the smooth planes of his stomach as her head lay on those perfect pecs.

But she kept her hands to herself until she remembered his offer from the night before.

Consider this me volunteering as tribute for you to explore to your heart's content.

Her hand glided over the muscles he'd obviously worked hard for, up and down. After two passes, his stomach tightened under her gentle touch, and his breathing hitched.

She checked his face to see green eyes soft with sleep staring down at her. "That tickles," he croaked, stifling a grin. She ripped her hand away, but he pulled it back. "I didn't say stop." He placed her hand firmly back on his chest and held it there. "Did you get some sleep?"

"Yeah," she said, blinking at him. "Thank you for staying last night." He'd kept her nightmares away.

He reached over and tucked some hair behind her ear. God, she must look a mess. "Anytime."

"You really mean that."

"I don't say things I don't mean." He lifted his arm and stretched, yawning. "As wonderful as this is, we should probably get up."

"Yeah." He thought this was wonderful? Josie's heart melted. She'd missed cuddling, not that her ex did it much after they moved in together.

"You want first crack at the bathroom?"

Suddenly her bladder had her attention. "I'll be quick." She threw back the covers and hopped out of bed.

The mirror showed her a frightening vision. Her hair had matted with sweat that had dried overnight, and the skin around her eyes still looked slightly red and puffy. Josie missed her skincare products. Somehow, she had to find some money and get new ones. She should have thought of that when Jenna had her order clothes online. Who knew when the FBI would finally let her know it was safe to go back into the real world?

She did her business on the toilet and brushed her teeth, then tried to brush her hair out. It was ridiculously long. When she'd first left with Brad, she'd cut it up to her shoulders, wanting to rid herself of one of the things that marked her parents' church. After the money dried up, she skipped the salon in favor of the grocery store. Seven months ago, she'd been in desperate need of a trim. Now it was dire.

She grunted as the brush caught in her strands when Finn knocked on the door. "Everything okay?"

Opening it, she let out a sigh. "Just trying to brush my hair. Go ahead." She sat back on the bed and continued to wrestle it into submission. Looked like she'd need to wash it again.

Finn finished in the bathroom and went to his own room to get dressed, she presumed. Her memories of the night before were a bit fuzzy. How had he ended up in her room?

She pulled on black leggings and a long tunic in green, tying her hair back in a ponytail. Then she knocked on his bedroom door. "Come in."

Finn turned to her as she pushed the door open. "Perfect timing. Can you help me with the stump sock?"

"Sure." As she pulled the compression material over his elbow, she asked the question on her mind. "Why did you come into my room last night?"

He ducked his head. "You were shouting, and it woke me. Took me a minute to figure out it was a nightmare, and not an intruder."

She shuddered. "I'm sorry."

"I'm not." Her head popped up at his vehemence. "I'd rather you wake me than deal with that on your own. I'm no stranger to shitty dreams."

She met his intense, knowing gaze, and her stomach flipped. He was a veteran, of course he knew nightmares. But she hated to think about what she might have said in her sleep. "Did I say anything... specific?"

He shook his head. "Just a lot of the word 'no.' And you had wrapped yourself up in that sheet like a straitjacket."

She nodded. Thank goodness. She wasn't ready for him to know the details of her past. Not yet. Maybe not ever.

"Let's get some breakfast." He popped his prosthesis on and tightened the straps. She led the way down the stairs and into the kitchen, where Jenna and Roger sat, arguing. Or rather, Jenna was arguing and Roger was sitting back and smirking while he poked the bear.

"What do you mean, you don't have any Christmas decorations?"

"Up until last month, it was just me here, Princess. And in case you haven't noticed, I don't have any neighbors to impress."

"And you already said you don't even put up a tree." Jenna huffed.

"Nope." He took a bite of his cereal. "We can change all that today if you want."

The redhead's ears perked up. "Really?"

"Sure. But we'll have to get literally everything. Mom and Dad have all the decorations and since I go over there every year, it just didn't matter."

"We're getting a real tree. I've never been allowed to decorate myself, so I want to do the whole nine yards."

"You did Christmas but never decorated?" Josie asked, her head tilted to one side. She and Finn sat at the bowls left for them in front of the empty stools at the island.

Jenna wrinkled her nose. "Mom always hired a professional decorator. I couldn't even *touch* the tree until Christmas morning when it came time to open presents."

Finn poured some cornflakes into his bowl and passed Josie the box. "That's no fun. I think Mom still puts up all the ornaments the four of us made in grade school."

Jenna laughed. "Yeah, those went into a box, never to be seen again. She probably trashed them when she thought I'd forgotten about them."

Josie's brow scrunched down. What a terrible mother.

Roger typed something on his phone and turned it around to show Jenna. "There's a tree farm along Highway 83. And the Christmas outlet isn't much farther."

"Smart location," commented Finn.

"We don't have anywhere to be today. Y'all want to come along?"

"I'd love to," Josie answered quickly. She ate breakfast while Jenna and Roger discussed where they were going to put the tree. Jenna wanted garland for the front of the house, as well. She tuned them out while they discussed how tall the tree should be.

She thought she was prepared for the amount of holiday cheer she was going to encounter. She was wrong.

They drove up a winding private road, through a verdant pine forest. At the end of the driveway stood a barn with the name Tree Haven painted in white over the huge sliding door. The tree farm sprawled across acres and acres, where the true enthusiasts could go cut down their own. Or, there were plenty in the barn already bagged up and labeled with height and the type of fir.

Inside, they had trees wrapped up in netting with labels like "Seven-foot Douglas Fir" and "Nine-foot Blue Spruce." The tabletop trees were absolutely adorable, and some even came predecorated with tiny colorful baubles. In the back was a coffee shop where they sold baked goods, fancy coffee, and hot chocolate.

"This place is amazing." Goose bumps prickled up the back of her neck, and she couldn't decide where to look first, so she tried to take it all in at once.

"Let's go chop down our own, Roger." Jenna needled him.

"What's wrong with the ones they've got up here?"

"But it's more immersive that way."

"Look, little Amazon, if you really want to chop it down ourselves, we can. But we still have to hit the outlet on our way home and you also wanted to decorate it tonight. This will save us time." When Jenna pouted, he wrapped an arm around her. "Next year, we'll come out the day after Thanksgiving and get the full experience. I promise."

"Really?"

"Really."

"Okay." Jenna pointed at a tree, which the worker tagged for them, and dragged Roger over to the wreaths hung up on the wall. "You need a wreath for the door, too."

He laughed and picked one out, while Josie wandered toward the shop in the back with Finn at her side.

"They're not very good at sticking with you."

She blushed. "I should be sticking with them," she muttered, gnawing on her lip. Things had been so calm, she had forgotten for a moment that she was under protection.

"Can I buy you a drink?"

"The peppermint hot chocolate sounds divine."

He ordered two, and with the lack of a line on a random Monday morning, they were served quickly. The first sip hit her tongue, and she moaned.

"Good?" One corner of Finn's mouth lifted in amusement.

"Amazing." She sipped it slowly as they made their way back toward the front, where Roger and the farm worker were loading the tree into the bed of the truck. They had to lay it diagonally and tie it in place to get it to fit.

"Where are we putting these ornaments, Bro?" Finn poked his brother.

"We'll fit them in somehow," he grumbled. "At least the wreath doesn't take up much space."

"Where'd you get those?" Jenna pointed at their cups.

"In the back." Finn answered her. "They have coffee and hot chocolate."

Josie sipped at her little cup of heaven and closed her eyes in bliss. "It's delicious."

"I'll be right back. Roger, do you want anything?"

"No, thanks. I'm good." He grinned at her retreating form.

Once Jenna had her drink and they were all piled in the truck, Roger headed back down the drive to the highway. At the next exit stood a billboard for Santa's Workshop Holiday Outlet, with a cartoon of the jolly man himself next to the text.

Santa's Workshop was decidedly busier than the tree farm. The giant parking lot was mostly full, but Roger found a place to park. She drained her hot chocolate while Finn came around to help her down from the truck.

"You spoil me," she murmured so the others couldn't hear.

"No." He shook his head. "I'm just demonstrating how you deserve to be treated."

"For the next guy, you mean?"

He looked away, red creeping up the back of his neck. "Something like that."

Disappointment was a rock in her gut. He might be attracted to her, but that didn't mean he wanted her for anything long-term. "I see." Taking a deep breath, she stepped between her bodyguards. Finn walked right behind her.

If he wasn't in this for the long-term, she wasn't sure she should start anything, no matter what her therapist's response to her email was. Even just having him teach her about pleasure seemed too intimate. Josie was a relationship girl. And maybe that was her problem. Finn had restarted her libido, and she really wanted to see where that took them. She intended to wait until she could stand on her own two feet before dating, but part of her wondered why didn't he want more?

Wait. How had she already become emotionally invested? They'd had one kiss!

It had to be the proximity, and his allergy to wearing a shirt.

The automatic doors swished open, and her jaw dropped as they stepped inside. Artificial trees created an indoor forest full of glittering lights. She wandered down the aisle, her mind absorbing all the different ornaments that hung from their branches. Some were color coordinated or decorated in a specific theme, like candy canes or peacocks, and each one had a sign with an aisle number where customers could buy the products shown.

"Wow," she breathed.

Jenna stood next to her. "This place is incredible."

The four of them strolled through the Christmas wonderland together, Jenna and Roger just up ahead. Along with what felt like half of Baltimore. She didn't want to get separated in such a busy store.

As she stopped to peer at a tree with bird ornaments, Finn pressed close. "Are you upset with me?"

She looked up into his face, filled with concern. "I just don't understand. You... made that offer last night. But you think we wouldn't work together?"

He had the good grace to look abashed. "Josie, you deserve better than a broken man."

She took a deep breath to temper her anger, so she didn't yell. "You're not *broken*, Finn. No more than I am." At that, his chin lifted in defiance. But before he could open his mouth, she raised a finger to his lips. "No, you're not. We've both been through some rough times, okay? Just because my scars are all on the inside doesn't make me more deserving, or a better partner."

His Adam's apple bobbed as he swallowed, and he looked like he might cry. "Would you... would you be with a guy with one arm?"

"I like you, Finn. I like you a *lot*. But I'm not ready for a relationship yet." Josie sighed. "When I date again..." She leaned in, lifting her chin so they were almost close enough to kiss. "I want someone who lets me make my own decisions. If we move in together, he'll share in the housework and cooking equally. I need someone patient in bed, because I don't know how I'm going to respond."

At that, his brows furrowed. Finn was no dummy. He could probably read between the lines. "How many arms he has doesn't make the list." She gulped. "I had someone once who had all his limbs intact. And he's how I ended up here."

Finn's eyes darted between hers, and he nodded. That's when Jenna hopped up next to them. "Hey, you guys, check out the inflatables!"

She led them further down the aisle, through a giant red and white striped archway that reminded her of the parade balloons. Josie couldn't remember the last time she'd smiled this much. How could she not? Penguins sliding down an igloo, Santa in a helicopter, of all things, and dozens of other characters lined the aisle.

Roger's shout made them break into a jog. Jenna got to him first. "What did you find?"

His face lit up like a little boy whose dreams had just come true. "They have Christmas dragons!" And indeed, they did. Three different ones, to be precise. One looked more like a traditional dragon, black with red accents. Its main nod to the season was the red present in its claws. The other two were bright green with red tummies and big, cartoon eyes. They both wore Santa hats, but one carried a red box with a bow and the other had candy canes. One in its hand, and one in its mouth.

"Roger..." Jenna's eyes lit with mischief. "They're perfect! We have to get these."

"I think I need one, too."

"You?" Roger looked at Finn in confusion.

"Hey, I'm eventually going to buy a place. If you're okay with it, I can put it up while I live with you."

Roger nodded and led them to the aisle where the inflatables lived while Jenna produced a cart from somewhere. The boxes nearly filled the cart, and they laughed as she went back for a second one.

They wandered the aisles, gathering lights for the tree, and outdoor lighted garland. "No white lights," Jenna said. "Multicolored only."

"Why?" asked Josie.

Jenna wrinkled her nose. "My mom only allowed white lights. She said multicolored lights were inelegant and childish."

"It's *Christmas*," Roger said, disgust dripping from his words. "You're supposed to act like a kid."

"Exactly! So I want to do all the garish decorating that I love and my mother would hate."

"Good thing she's not invited."

Finn insisted she pick out an ornament to commemorate her first holiday in Baltimore. Josie gravitated toward the bird themed aisle, floating down it with Finn at her side. She considered the options. They had ceramic birds, glass birds, birds in cages, birds on a branch. But then she found little feathered friends that would clip onto the branches, like they were real. Like they were free.

Lifting the card in her hands, she stroked their little feathered heads, thinking about how she hoped for freedom for the girls still held captive. Something about putting these on the tree felt like keeping hope alive, like a prayer. She turned and placed them on top of the inflatable dragon with the candy canes that Finn had declared was his.

"That's not much, sweetheart."

"I like them. And the tree is going to be so full once Jenna gets done with it."

"True." He looked over at the second cart piled high with garland, lights, and the wildest variety of ornaments anyone had probably seen. Jenna had even found a Santa hat with a fake beard attached that she'd held up to Roger, then stuffed in the cart.

After Roger and Jenna finally picked a star for the top of the tree, the four of them got in a line that wrapped halfway around the store. As they waited their turn, Finn slipped his good arm around Josie's waist. She leaned her head on his shoulder. Her gaze wandered over the patrons in the store until it snagged on a familiar head of dark hair.

Her spine stiffened. A quick inhale through her nose was the only sound she dared make. It couldn't be... could it?

"Sunshine? What's wrong?" Finn's arm tightened around her. Roger and Jenna took note of her body language and slipped into protection mode, putting themselves between her and the rest of the store.

The knowledge they were carrying weapons didn't ease her mind like she thought it would. How could they discharge them in a crowded store like this?

She held her breath as the dark-haired apparition of her ex, Brad, disappeared down an aisle without turning in her direction. Only then did she breathe.

Jenna, fierce, short, Jenna, glared up at her. "Did you see someone?"

"I'm not sure. It looked like my ex." Jenna and Roger had been there when she gave Agent Patterson her story.

They knew Brad had been the one to sell her to the syndicate. But he should still be in Montana.

"It can't be him. I have to be overreacting." But Jenna and Finn weren't convinced.

"Roger, we need to get her out of here."

"Give me your card and I'll pay for both our stuff." Finn held out his hand. Roger slapped a card into it and the three of them hightailed it back to the truck.

Roger circled the vehicle, checking for what, she wasn't sure. They bundled her into the backseat, and she sank to the floor. She hugged her arms to herself, shivering despite the heater in the truck.

It took ages for Finn to get back to them, but once they were out of the parking lot, Roger declared it safe, and she could sit up and buckle her seat belt. Finn pulled her into the middle seat and wrapped his arm around her.

"I'm sorry," she whispered. He pressed his lips to her temple.

"It's all good, Sunshine." She expected questions. But when she turned to look at him, all she saw was affection.

"Relax."

The adrenaline bled out of her and she nodded off against his shoulder.

Chapter 18

"DAMN THIS WIND!" ROGER cursed again as he and Finn struggled to get their new inflatable decorations tethered to the ground. He held onto the eight-foot oversized balloon while Roger tried to push the peg in to the lawn.

"Maybe next time we should wait to inflate them until we've got the pegs in?" He laughed as Roger flipped his middle finger up.

Finally, two bright green Christmas dragons stood between the house and the detached garage. Once they got the boys settled, they headed around to the front porch where Jenna had wrapped the garland around the railing. She'd put another section around the door, both with colorful lights that connected to an app on her phone. Currently they were running a candy cane stripe design. It matched the three-foot lighted candy canes she'd lined along the walkway.

The wreath she'd insisted on hung on the door. The girls were warm inside, organizing the ornaments. He followed Roger as he stomped into the foyer and kicked off his shoes.

"Alright, the outside is done. Let's get this tree decorated," Roger declared.

Finn groaned, looking at the beast they'd hauled in from the truck. "It's crooked again."

"Did we get a bad stand?"

"I don't know." He held it in place with Ken, his prosthetic arm, once more, as Roger turned the screws so it was straight. One benefit to this arm was not getting pricked by the tree's needles.

"Alright, that should do it." Jenna and Josie wandered in from the kitchen, looking cozy with mugs of something hot.

"More hot chocolate?" He grinned at Josie. His sunshine sure had a sweet tooth.

She nodded and sipped some more.

"I had it in the grocery order." Jenna explained when Roger looked at her funny. "What?"

"Why did you need a grocery order?"

"Because after we're done with this, I want to make cookies!"

Roger just shook his head. "Let's get started, then."

Jenna tuned the TV into a holiday music station, and they got to work. Josie watched them for a bit but took to decorating the tree like a fish to water. When they were done, it looked like the Christmas store had exploded onto the tree.

"Now we place the star?" Josie held up the glittering gold topper in her hand.

"Nope!" Jenna grinned. "Now we do the tinsel!" She pulled out two packages of the old-fashioned strand tinsel and opened them up. "You just toss it on the branches like so." She demonstrated with a flick of her wrist.

Josie tried but ended up with a giant clump on the tree. She pulled it off and tried again.

Roger, however, gave a mischievous smirk and tossed his tinsel onto Jenna.

"Hey!" She retaliated and tossed tinsel at his head.

Not one to miss the fun, Finn flung his at Josie. They caught in her hair, and she gasped, then threw hers at him. It caught on his sweatshirt and suddenly the four of them broke out into a tinsel fight, laughing the whole time.

When they ran out of tinsel and breath, they collapsed on the couch. "I think we got more tinsel on us than the tree!" Josie said with a giggle. Jenna picked up what strands she could salvage and draped them on the bare spots in the tree. After that she spied Josie's birds.

"Josie! You should clip your birds up."

"Okay."

"You still want to bake cookies, Princess?" Roger asked, exhaustion written on his face.

"Yes! Don't worry, you won't have to do a thing." Roger grunted and handed Finn the star.

"You want to do the honors?"

Finn waved it away. "Bro, it's your first tree on your own. You should do it."

"But that involves getting up."

"Come on." Finn mock-scowled at him. "You'll regret it if you don't."

"Fine." He pulled himself off the couch and placed the star as Josie clipped on her last bird.

"We have the craziest tree ever." Jenna said, her hands on her hips. "And I *love* it."

"Good. Now I'm going to order dinner while you start the cookies."

Jenna saluted her boyfriend and pulled Josie into the kitchen with her.

Roger stared after Jenna, but Finn watched his brother. "That's a good look on you, man."

He furrowed his brows as he swept more tinsel off his shoulder. "What is? Tinsel?"

"No," Finn chuckled. "Happiness."

Roger smiled to himself and reached over to where Finn sat in the recliner. "It would look good on you too, if you wanted to let it in." He patted him on the shoulder and sat back on the couch.

Finn looked back to where the girls had disappeared. The sounds of bowls and utensils echoed from the kitchen. "I don't even know what that would look like anymore."

"I didn't expect her at all. I thought I was happy. But it turned out I wasn't. Not like I realized I could be." Roger smiled at something in his own head. "Sometimes love just smacks you upside the head when you're not looking."

Finn cringed and laughed. "Don't ever go into business as a love guru. Keep your day job."

THE FOLLOWING DAY WAS the day he'd agreed to talk to his alma mater's rifle team. Coach Atkins welcomed him at the range, handed him some earplugs and led him back to the section the kids practiced in.

"Thanks for dropping by, Finn. The kids are looking forward to this."

"You're welcome, Coach. It feels weird being back here." The more things changed, the more they stayed the same. While the faces around the range were fresh, it still looked the same as when he'd been in high school. Cement walls echoed the sound of bullets flying. The private room that Coach rented for the team held about a dozen teenagers, gangly pimply creatures too old to be children but too inexperienced to be considered adults. Coach gave the signal to cease fire. The kids laid down their weapons and took their ear protection off.

"Everyone, I want you to meet a former student who served as the boys' team captain back in the day. This is Finn Hunt." Coach slapped a hand on his shoulder and Finn waved at the kids, who greeted him in that lackluster manner that teens have. "Finn took the top score in the state competition his senior year."

An awed hush stole over the kids. Their wide eyes fixated on him now.

"I didn't think you'd remember that, Coach."

"Of course I remember it. I've got the photo framed on the wall in my office." When he wasn't coaching the rifle team, he taught gym at the high school.

"What happened to your arm?" One of the kids called out. Finn wasn't sure which.

"After that state competition, the Marines recruited me. I was a sniper for them the past ten years." He lifted Ken, showing him off to the kids in the back. "But my career was cut short by a roadside bomb."

A chorus of "aw man" and "that sucks" made one side of his mouth tilt up. Adults pitied you; kids were generally more accepting. Then someone else spoke out.

"Why don't you have an arm like Timmy?"

He shrugged. "This is what the doctor gave me." Wait, one of the kids had a prosthetic arm? "What do you mean?"

A short boy came forward, one he hadn't seen over the taller kids on the team. He pushed his sleeve back to reveal a sleek metal arm that went all the way to his shoulder.

"That looks awesome." Finn crouched to get a better look.

Timmy demonstrated his full range of motion, even flexing his individual fingers, something Finn's arm couldn't do. "It's bionic."

"You can shoot with that?"

He nodded.

"Wow." Finn's mind whirled with the possibilities. He'd never get his old job back, but taking one with Roger might be a possibility if he had an arm like that.

Timmy pulled his sleeve down. "I never had an arm there. I was born without one."

"It's only been a month or so for me."

"You lost your job because you had no arm?" Timmy's brow furrowed.

"The arm wasn't the only thing damaged, just the most obvious. You need to have perfect vision to be a sniper. And the blast damaged my corneas."

"We used to call him Eagle Eye." Coach said with a chuckle.

Finn stood back up. "That carried over into the Marines, by the way."

Coach laughed and slapped his shoulder again. "You should look into one of those arms, Finn. The VA didn't do you any favors."

He looked down at the arm he'd named after a plastic doll. "I will."

"Alright kids, back to practice. Let's show Eagle Eye how we're carrying on the Bulldog legacy!"

"It was incredible. The kid had full range of motion, even his fingers. I watched him shoot just fine with it." Finn shoveled more macaroni into his mouth at his parents' dinner table.

"That sounds incredible, Finn. You should see about getting one," his mother encouraged him.

Nadia cleared her throat and made a face at their mother. "I've heard of them, too. They're pricey though."

"But it sounds like an amazing idea, Finn!" Mom and Nadia eyed each other, having a private conversation with their eyes.

It wasn't like Nadia to be cagey like this. What the hell was going on?

Shaking his head, he followed Roger out to the kitchen to get more drinks. "If I can get one of those bionic arms, I can shoot again."

"Really? Oh wait, that makes sense since the kid was on the team."

"Yeah. He said his dad works for the company. I sent an email. Hopefully, they call me soon."

"They might be a bit busy with the holidays."

"True. But I'm not going anywhere." At Roger's chuckle, he shook his head. "I will get my own place soon, though. I don't want to mooch off you indefinitely."

"Finn, you're welcome to stay. I think being around people has been good for you. So whenever you're ready, that's fine."

"Thanks, Bro."

Josie wandered into the kitchen with some of the plates. His mom had balked at first, but now that she'd been coming with Roger and Jenna for a while she had just about been adopted as one of the family. Unfortunately, with either Roger or Jenna always being in the house, that meant little alone time. He hadn't had a chance to talk to her alone since they put up the tree, but he was dying to kiss her again. And no way in hell had he wanted to knock on her door like a creeper when she was going to bed.

Although if that was the only time he had, he'd try it later tonight.

Luckily, Roger slipped back to the dining room to get more dishes. But Josie stayed on the other side of the island.

"Come on, Sunshine, I don't bite."

She shook her head. "The mistletoe is still up there."

Finn looked up. So it was. "Yup. Mom doesn't usually take it down till New Year's." He leaned back against the counter, daring her to come kiss him again. Desire flashed across her face, arcing through the air. But she shook her head once more.

"Not with an audience."

"Okay." That was totally fair. He stepped away from the offending plant and came around to her side of the barrier. "Tonight?" he murmured in her ear, and didn't miss the shiver that traveled down her spine. She nodded in agreement.

Now he just had to get through dessert with his family.

Chapter 19

SHE WAS GOING TO do it. She was going to ask him tonight.

Nodding at herself in the mirror, Josie thought back to the enthusiastic response her therapist had at Finn's offer. It only strengthened her conviction as she shivered in her short satin nightgown. Jenna had told her to order clothes on her card, and she had snuck this into the order alongside the warm pajamas and sweaters for winter. She loved the lavender color on her pale skin, how it made her gray eyes look ethereal. Like she wasn't a human at all; she was a fae from the other realm that could seduce Finn to follow her through the fairy ring.

Maybe she'd been reading too many of those fantasy romances on Frankie's library account.

She shook her head and brushed her blonde hair once more. "Now or never," she whispered to herself. Her nipples pebbled through the thin satin. Finn had better warm her up.

She'd shaved her legs, trimmed her bikini line. Josie was as ready as she could be. Knocking gently on the door to his room, she opened it when she heard him say, "Come in."

He stopped in the middle of taking his arm off, and stared. She padded into the room on bare feet, shutting the bathroom door behind her. His throat bobbed and his mouth moved as if he wanted to speak but couldn't form the words.

Feeling emboldened, Josie opened the moisturizer on his nightstand. "Can I help?"

When he nodded, she pushed at his shoulder, and he sat on the bed. That put him at eye-level with her breasts, but he was staring at her face. As she worked the moisturizer into his scar tissue, she willed him to look at them. With a shy side-glance, Josie realized she was going to have to spell it out for him. Even though her libido was frustrated at that, her heart warmed. He was a good man, and he wouldn't take anything she wasn't willing to give.

Which just made her want to give him everything. "You can look."

"I'm sure they're lovely. But your face..." He reached up and cupped her cheek. "Your confidence is breathtaking."

She nuzzled his hand as she finished the massage. "I want to..." *Come on, say it.* "I want to have sex with you."

Her brows furrowed when he didn't immediately take over. "Did you hear me?"

"I heard you, Sunshine. But I don't want to jump into something you might not be ready for." With a sigh, she remembered what she'd told him in the Christmas store. That she didn't know how she'd react to a man in her bed.

"Why don't we start off slow?"

She whined in frustration. It had been hard enough to say the first time.

"Come down here and kiss me. We can play it by ear."

God, she was so horny. Weeks of living with this hot, sweet Marine twenty-four-seven had driven her dormant libido to distraction.

And damn, she'd missed kissing.

She slid onto his lap and his left arm banded around her back. Her arms wrapped around his neck and she pressed her mouth to his.

He let her lead for about five seconds before he took over the kiss. *Yes.* She needed him to want her. To feel like she was still desirable after what she'd been through.

The satin rubbed against her sensitive flesh, and she pressed closer. He broke the kiss with a groan.

"Baby, that's sexy as hell. Rub all over me." He laid back, pulling her with him. She'd never been on top during sex. Sitting up, she moved to take the straps of her nightie down, but he stopped her.

"Leave it on. We can work up to more later. The point of this is to make you feel good." He gazed up at her with hooded eyes. That's when she realized where she was sitting. His sweatpants didn't restrain his bulge, and her panties got damp as she registered it between her legs.

"What do you like?"

She shrugged. "No one's asked that before." Her cheeks heated, but she didn't look away from his grimace.

"Do what feels good. If I say or do something that doesn't achieve that, just tell me. Okay?" She nodded. "I don't have a lot of blood in my brain right now, so keep it simple." His voice sounded strained.

"I will." She leaned over and electricity shot up her spine from where they rubbed together. Her mouth dropped open as she brought her face down to his. "I like kissing you." Then she sealed her mouth over his.

She swallowed his moans as she pressed their bodies together. Her hips moved of their own accord, sending pulses of pleasure through her nether regions as she ground against him. The rasp of his stubble against her cheek led her to draw a line of kisses to his ear, nibbling on the lobe. Her hands explored his chest as she kissed down his neck. For the first time she could remember, she had all the power.

With his mouth unoccupied, Finn started spouting.

"Yeah, baby, that feels so good. Rub all over me. I feel how hot you are. Rub that needy little pussy all over my cock. God, I haven't come in my pants since I was a teenager."

His words made her focus on the sensations between her legs, and she gasped as his hardness rubbed over her clit. She needed a better angle. Sitting up, she pressed her hands into his pecs, pushing her breasts together and nearly making them pop out of the triangles of fabric holding them in. Shifting back—there. Oh God, he was big. And hard. And ... all hers.

She closed her eyes and focused on the feeling between her legs. The matching panties were likely ruined, and she suspected she was leaving a wet spot on his pants, but she didn't care. Back and forth, back and forth. She spiraled higher and higher but couldn't quite push herself over the edge.

"Touch me," she gasped out. Finn lifted his hand, and she grabbed it, pressing it to her breast.

"Fuck, you're so hot." His hand cupped her through the satin, and his thumb rolled over the hard peak of her nipple, the fabric gliding over the sensitive flesh and making her pussy clench. She lifted a hand to tease the other one, when Finn sat up and closed his mouth over her other nipple and sucked through the fabric.

That did it. She detonated for the first time in years, convulsing in his lap. Her body went lax, and she slumped against him as aftershocks twitched through her.

He brought her back down to the bed with him, his arm wrapped around her again, but this time to soothe and bring her down to Earth.

"That was..."

"Incredible," she supplied. She blinked tears away as she realized she wasn't broken. The months of enslavement to the syndicate hadn't stolen this. She could still feel pleasure.

"I need to go take care of something," Finn grunted.

"Oh! Let me." She scrambled off him, but his cheeks turned pink as he shook his head.

"Not like that. I, uh, I just need to change my pants."

Josie's eyes widened, and she covered her mouth with her hand to hold in her giggles. He'd come in his pants *because of her*! This big, bad ass Marine had orgasmed just from her dry humping him.

Finn sheepishly rose and grabbed some things from the dresser Roger had put in here when he'd decided to make Finn a room. Then he escaped into the bathroom to change.

She didn't want to assume he'd want her to stay, but it was chilly outside the blanket. Maybe she should sneak back to her room? But she'd have to go out into the hallway and she might run into Roger. Before she could get the guts to leave, Finn returned.

"Are you staying?"

"Do you want me to?"

He nodded. "I liked it when we slept together before."

"I did, too." Sleeping next to him had made her feel protected for the first time; truly safe. Josie slipped under the blanket, and he followed, curling around her body with his left arm, holding her close.

"Good night, Josie."

She smiled and turned out the light. "Good night, Finn."

FINALLY, IT WAS TIME to see what *Dungeons and Dragons* was all about.

Finn had helped her put her character together and explained how the game worked. But Jon had needed more time to put his campaign together. So now, the week before Christmas, the five of them gathered around Roger's rarely used dining room table, dice in hand.

"Here's the setup. You've all been summoned by this village's elders from neighboring towns to help them solve a problem." Jon rubbed his hands together, and took on the voice of the elder statesman.

"Thank you for answering my call, adventurers. We have asked you here today to help us with a monumental job. The tale of Hansel and Gretel, two children who escaped the evil witch Grizelda, has passed down many generations. Most people don't realize that the children called our village home. The witch has been quiet for years, but lately children have gone ... missing."

"Missing?" Josie leaned across the table.

"And you think this witch is to blame?" Roger asked.

Jon nodded gravely. "Precisely. She blames us for destroying the last Candy Cottage and freeing the children she'd turned into gingerbread."

"I thought she just ate them," Josie interrupted.

"A common misinterpretation, and one I admit, we did not deter. Because if we could save even one child from being captured, it would be worth the scare to them." Jon sighed. "But the hunters returned last week saying that the Candy Cottage has been spotted deep in the woods once more, and children have been going missing for a month. We cannot allow Grizelda to terrorize our village again! If you bring us her head, we will reward you handsomely."

Once the characters all agreed, they left the town hall in search of clues. Jenna's rogue character spied a trail of crumbs leading into the woods, and they followed. They came across a pair of goblins, who Finn insisted on spying on, and they overheard how the witch had hired the goblins to patrol the woods and alert her if the adults got too close to the Candy Cottage.

The game captivated Josie, and the hours fell away as they played on that rainy evening. Before she knew it, the game wrapped up and Jon was saying his goodbyes.

"How's work?" Roger asked him.

Jon pinched the bridge of his nose. "I don't know how much longer I can stand it, to be honest."

"Seriously?" Finn asked, taking a swig of his Dr Pepper.

"Yeah, the stress is no joke. I feel like I'm looking at a heart attack or something in the next ten years." He rubbed the back of his head. "I've got nineteen years in, though. Next year, I can retire. And I'm going to." He pulled his boots on and tied them up. "Stick a fork in me, I'm done."

"Good for you." Roger slapped him on the shoulder. "You deserve a break."

"Thanks." He shrugged into his jacket and gave them all a wave. "See you guys for Christmas."

Roger's phone pinged with a text. "Sam says he and Frankie will be back in town for Christmas. I'll tell him to plan to eat with us at Mom and Dad's." He typed away as they lounged around the table.

"Can you ask if he's heard anything from Ross?" Josie asked, biting her lip. No word had come from the FBI agent handling her case, and her restrictions were starting to chafe. She wanted to get a job and get her own place so she could date Finn for real, instead of... whatever they were doing.

"Who's Ross?" Finn asked quickly.

"He's Sam's friend from the FBI," Roger answered as he typed. "He took Josie's case since Sam is cybercrimes and couldn't do it himself."

Finn grunted an acknowledgment. Jenna just grinned wickedly at them. She winked at Josie, and Josie immediately felt her cheeks turn red. Jenna must know something was up between them.

The little instigator chimed in. "Yeah, we all ate dinner with him and his girlfriend after we gave our statements."

Her surly Marine's demeanor relaxed at that. "Statements?"

Roger shook his head at Jenna. "Not our story to tell, little Amazon."

"It kind of is." Josie turned to Roger. "If you want to tell him your side of it, that's fine. It'd be nice not to have to retell mine again."

Roger scrutinized her, but nodded in understanding. "Okay, Josie. If that's what you want."

She nodded. Once Finn heard what had happened to her, he'd understand she couldn't take on a man until she'd healed from her ordeal.

"Did you take a pain pill recently?" Roger asked Finn.

"No. Not yet."

"I'll grab you a beer. You're going to want one for this conversation."

"Why don't we sit in the living room where it's comfortable?" Jenna tilted her head at Josie. She followed the petite redhead, but wasn't sure where to sit. Should she sit in the recliner so she wouldn't be sitting next to Finn? No, that would mean he'd be looking at her, and she wasn't sure she could take it.

Jenna sat in the middle of the couch and patted the end next to her. Josie's grateful smile wobbled. She'd never had someone take her under their wing as a friend as quickly as Jenna and Frankie had. She only hoped she'd been able to give the same comfort to the other girls while she was held captive.

When Roger came back with two beers, he handed one to Finn, who'd sat on the other end of the couch from Josie. Roger took the armchair, and then he explained how Jenna's friend Frankie had shown up asking for help to take down a human trafficking ring run by the syndicate they used to work for. Jenna had got out, and Frankie had followed, but not before finding evidence of their evil business.

She thanked Jenna profusely in her head that she didn't have to sit next to Finn while Jenna and Roger alternated, telling the story of how they'd broken into the house and tried to rescue all the victims. That they'd only found her. And that the FBI was now investigating and trying to take down the syndicate, who had left Josie behind when they ran.

"Since she didn't want to go into witness protection, Ross said she could stay with us under our protection. That's why we can't leave her alone."

Finn chugged the rest of his beer and stood. "Josie…" She looked up at him from the couch, and while she expected sympathy, pity even, what she saw was devastation on his face. His red-rimmed eyes locked onto her, and his whole body vibrated with tension.

"Were they the ones that hit you?"

He'd seen her reaction to his outburst that night. She'd told him not to touch her. Of course, he'd figured it out. "Not the only ones," she admitted with a sigh. Even Jenna and Roger knew that part. She appreciated Roger not telling Finn about her ex's betrayal, even though they knew about it from being present during her statement to Ross.

"My boyfriend… ex-boyfriend… he used to hit me. After I gave up my family and my home to go with him. I was planning to leave him as soon as I got a job, but I didn't get to sit for the test."

"Why?" he croaked, and his jaw clenched.

Josie looked away. "Because my boyfriend sold me to the syndicate."

His sharp inhale cut across the silent room. "Rog, you still got that heavy bag downstairs?" Roger must have nodded, because Finn's arm clicked open and he laid it down on the coffee table. "If I'm not back in an hour, come get me."

Jenna's brow furrowed as Finn disappeared into the basement. "Roger, is that safe? I thought you needed someone to hold the heavy bag during a workout."

"You do." Roger finished his beer and collected the empties. "I'll go down in a few minutes and make sure he doesn't knock himself on his ass."

"Good plan."

"Why wouldn't he ask Roger to come down and help?" Josie didn't understand what was going on.

"From what I've gathered about Finn, he's mad and he wants to hurt someone that's not here. So instead, he's going to hurt himself." Jenna shrugged. "Guys are weird, sometimes."

Roger returned from taking the recycling out to the bin and waved as he headed downstairs. A heavy thumping sound echoed up the basement stairs until he shut the door behind him.

That night, a freshly showered Finn took the unlocked door as the invitation she'd meant it to be, and crawled into bed behind her. She turned and snuggled into him before he could even ask permission. The last things she felt before sleep took her was his arm wrapping around her and his kiss on her head.

237

Chapter 20

"THANKS," FINN SAID AS Josie rolled the stump sock up his arm again in the morning.

"You're welcome." She lingered near him, a question written all over her face. Josie hadn't tried to touch Finn intimately again since she'd told him why she needed protecting a few days ago. She pulled him into her bedroom night after night, just to hold her, but she hadn't made another move since. Maybe she sensed that he just needed some time to wrap his head around it. But that was only partly the reason.

Because the fact was, he was falling for her.

They took turns cooking for the house and she showed him cleaning tricks the Marines would never think of. It was delightfully domestic and everything he'd wanted in a partner.

At night she did the stump massage for him, and he went to bed with a stiff dick. And every morning she helped him with the stump sock. Doctor Lopez was pleased at the last appointment and said that he could get a better, newer prosthesis now that the stump had shrunk. Finn was looking into the bionic arm like he'd seen on Timmy from the rifle team, and they were crazy expensive. But they had attachments that would let him work out again.

He liked it when Josie hung off his arm.

"What is it?" Finn put on his prosthesis to hide how desperately he wanted to pull her into his arms and kiss her.

"Are you upset with me?"

His heart dropped. "Why would I be upset with you?"

"Because... because I didn't tell you before. Because I can't commit yet. Because I'm... damaged."

Now he threw all his thoughts of "letting her come to him" out the window and wrapped his arms around her. Using Ken was a little awkward, but he didn't care. "Sunshine, you are not damaged. Not at all. I don't care about your history, only that they hurt you and that makes me want to hurt *them*." She hugged him back, squeezing his waist. "It's your story to tell and you decide who to tell and when. Thank you for trusting me enough to tell me."

"You're welcome. I'm sorry it took so long. I just... I didn't want you to treat me differently."

He'd had an idea late one night when he couldn't sleep, thanks to his hard-on and decided when she was ready, that would be the next thing he'd teach her about pleasure. It sounded like she was ready to him.

"Question for you. Anyone ever eat your pussy?"

Josie turned bright red, and he smothered a grin. He'd learned his girl liked dirty talk, but it made her blush something fierce. "N-n-no..."

"Second lesson. Tonight, I want you to ride my face."

Her gray eyes widened. "Won't I smother you?"

In answer, Finn lifted her up with his left arm. "I think I'll manage."

His Sunshine stared down at him through hooded eyes, and her arms wrapped around his neck.

"Did you like what we did last time?"

"Uh-huh." She licked her lips. "I really liked it when your mouth was on my breast."

"You did, huh?"

She leaned forward, grazing his nose with hers. "Uh-huh."

Sensing the mood shift, his voice dropped to a husky whisper. "I like when you tell me those things." The lust burning in her eyes made him feel like a king. *He* brought that out in her. Someone who had every reason to never want a man's touch again wanted *him*. "You want more of that?"

"Mmhmm." She kissed him, those sultry lips parting his as her tongue danced inside his mouth.

He fell back onto the bed, closing his eyes as Josie writhed on his lap and kissed him senseless.

Fuck it if she wasn't ready for a relationship yet. He'd wait forever.

She pulled away, and he chased her, but she giggled and sat up. His cock was at attention beneath her, and when Finn opened his eyes, she was biting her lip with a mischievous look on her face.

"Can we do what we did before? Just with one change?"

"Anything you want, baby." She could ask him for anything.

Josie's slender fingers went to the buttons on her adorable snowman pajamas and slowly started to undo them. "Is this okay?"

"Fuck, yes." He grabbed onto her hip and bucked as she revealed two perky round tits he was going to get his hand and mouth all over. Finn licked his lips, and she dropped the shirt from her shoulders. "Is that pussy needy this morning?"

She shuddered. "God, the way you talk. It's so… naughty."

"But I make you feel nice, right?"

She nodded.

"That's all I care about." He pressed his hand on her back and encouraged to lean over. "Now put those gorgeous tits in my face and get off on my dick."

Josie writhed and whined, pushing against him harder when he rolled one nipple under his thumb and sucked on the other. She must have been as desperate as he'd been these past few days, because it took no time before she was shaking on top of him.

"Finn! Yes! *Finn!*"

He couldn't wait for tonight.

NADIA KNOCKED ON THE door after lunch and Roger let her in. "What's up, Sis? You're not working?"

"Nah, I took the day off." She kicked the snow off her shoes but left her coat on. "By the way, I love the decorations. I sent pictures to the girls."

Jenna called out from the kitchen. "Hey, Nad. What's up?"

"I'm kidnapping Finn."

Finn looked up from where he sat next to Josie. "Hard to kidnap me when I'm bigger than you, and you already said you wanted to hang out." He laughed. "Where are we going?"

"It's a surprise." She pushed up her black glasses and grinned. "Come on, big brother, trust me?"

He narrowed his eyes. "Did Mom put you up to this?"

"No! She didn't know anything about it." Then she mumbled something under her breath.

"What was that?"

"Nothing! But I need to steal you, and we need to leave now."

"Alright. Let me get my shoes."

Josie looked up at him with a soft smile and murmured, "Have fun."

His heart swelled with affection. "I'll see you tonight." He winked, and she blushed. What they'd done that morning should tide them over, but he couldn't wait to show her the pleasures of receiving oral.

With his shoes and coat on, Finn followed Nadia to her little Chevy. "I miss driving."

"But for once I get to drive *you* around!" she sassed. Finn chuckled at the memories of carting her to the mall when she was in middle school and he was a senior. "Come on, you taught me to drive. You know I'm a good driver."

"Well, if you're not anymore, I'm going to blame Caleb."

Nadia threw her head back and laughed. She expertly handled the three-point turn to get back to the street, and Finn relaxed.

"We haven't been out, just the two of us in years."

"I know. Now that you're home, maybe we can more often." She smiled as she flipped her turn signal and turned out of Roger's long gravel driveway.

"Yeah. I need to get some Christmas shopping done."

"After our appointment.""Appointment?"

"You'll see."

She wouldn't tell him anything else for the rest of the trip, driving them to a part of Baltimore he didn't recognize. When she pulled into a parking lot behind a squat cement block building, he still didn't understand.

"What is this place?"

"Let's go in and find out."

It turned out to be an office building. Nadia directed him to suite 150, where she walked up to a check-in desk while he sat in an empty waiting room. After speaking with the receptionist, she sat down next to him, vibrating with excitement.

"Nadia, this looks like a doctor's office."

"Yup."

Why the hell would his sister bring him to a doctor's appointment... oh fuck no. "Nadia, are you... You're pregnant?" He stood up, prepared to knock her fiancé into next week. "That's it. I'm gonna kill him."

"What? No!" She grabbed onto Finn's arm and yanked him back down to the chair. "God, Finn, no, I'm not pregnant. And if I was, why would I want you here and not my fiancé?" She slapped a hand over her forehead. "Jesus Christ."

"Then what am I doing here, Nadia?"

The door opened and a woman in scrubs called out, "Finley Hunt?"

Nadia stood with him and dragged him to the door. "Come on, I'll explain."

The nurse led them to a room with physical therapy equipment and a table with chairs. "We'll be with you in just a minute."

Finn didn't sit, but he pointed at a chair for Nadia. "Sit. And start talking."

She sighed and fell into the chair, her chestnut ponytail swaying with the motion. "You don't have to loom over me, Finn. I'll tell you."

He was too agitated to sit, though, and just motioned for her to continue.

"When we heard about your injury, I mentioned it to the squad. I didn't think you'd care, since we tell each other everything." He nodded. Those girls were the sisters she'd never had.

"Rosie went into research mode and found out about all the advancements in bionic limbs for people with limb differences. She looked into who had the best outcomes and technology. Good thing she can read all those reports. God knows the medical terminology makes my eyes bleed." Nadia waved her hand in the air, probably flustered at his stony expression. "Anyway, she recommended this company, but the costs were really high. Most of their patients have to apply for grants or set up crowdfunding to afford it, even though they make it as affordable as possible without compromising the quality."

She took a breath, and he furrowed his brows. Had the girls paid for this themselves?

"So I took some pictures from Mom of you in your uniform. Olivia helped with the graphics, Mia helped me write up the story for the crowdfunding campaign, and then everyone shared the hell out of the web page. Mia's Hollywood contacts got involved, and well..." She blushed. His little will-kick-your-ass-with-a-sword sister was blushing? "Let's just say you can probably get as many accessories as you want."

Finn froze, a ringing in his ears that sounded distinctly like sleigh bells. He fell into the chair opposite her. "You... you guys are paying for this?"

She shook her head. "Not by ourselves. We all chipped in, yeah, but we knew we'd need help." Then she shrugged. "Merry Christmas?"

Finn rubbed his eyes as a laugh stuttered out of him. "Hell of a Christmas present, baby sister."

Nadia accepted his hug with a grunt. "The girls all wanted to be here, but I didn't want to overwhelm you. Also, I was the one that had to set up the appointment since I'm related."

Tears. Tears were leaking from his eyes, and he wiped them away. "How did Mom give birth to one baby girl, yet I ended up with five nosy sisters?" They laughed. "Did Mom know?"

She shook her head. "Not until after dinner that night. I had to tell her so she would keep her mouth shut."

Finn managed to get himself together before the doctor came in. "Hello, Mr. Hunt. Ready to see your new arm?"

"Hell yeah," he croaked, taking Ken off and laying it on the table. "Let's get me fitted, Doc."

Chapter 21

The control was incredible. They'd mapped his nerves with some kind of machine and that was how the arm was controlled. Finn didn't fully understand it, but when he'd asked about working out again, the doctor made a note that he needed a certain attachment for the final limb.

This one was a loaner until they finished manufacturing the final one in the shop.

He'd spent the afternoon learning how to control the new arm. Doctor Hurst even brought out an old Nintendo system with *Duck Hunt* to showcase the arm's control.

Nadia had taken a video and sent it to her squad so they could see their efforts paying off.

Finn could shoot again.

They discussed colors and helped him download the app to his phone that would let him program the arm for different activities. That was how he could turn the light on it different colors, dim it, or turn it off completely.

Nadia and he left with a bag holding Ken the plastic arm, informational booklets, and the special charging station for the new arm. He'd come back after the new year for more appointments and fittings. And his sister had arranged everything.

"Thank you," he said with his arm around her shoulders. "You're the best sister a guy could have."

"I'm just glad we got you back." Nadia hugged him tightly. "Now," she wiped tears from under her glasses. "You said you had shopping to do. Let's hit the food court and the mall. I'm starving."

"Sounds good. I need an idea for Josie."

Three days before Christmas, the mall was a zoo. Nadia only got a parking spot because someone else was leaving. They picked their dinner by the shortest line, getting sub sandwiches. He brushed the debris from previous customers off a small two-seat table in the corner and they devoured their food.

"So, Josie, huh?" Nadia asked with a smirk.

"You've got mayo on your chin," was all he answered. But then he sighed. He was tired of hiding it. "Yeah. I ... I really like her, Nad." His heart raced in his chest. Like wasn't strong enough of a word, but he couldn't bring himself to admit he was leaning toward the L word to someone else first. She should be the first to know, not his sister.

"What kind of present are you looking for? Jewelry?"

It wasn't a bad idea. "I'm not sure we're there yet. She says she's not ready for a relationship."

"Do you know why she's staying with Roger and Jenna?" Nadia tore open her chips.

"It's not my place to say. But she's waiting to take her test to be a nurse."

"Oh! I know the perfect thing."

"Really?" He licked onion dressing off his fingers and wiped them carefully with the napkin.

"Yeah, this mall has a scrub store Rosie loves. She buys all her scrubs there. You could get her a gift card, so she won't have to worry about buying her uniform."

"Wait... how do you...?"

Nadia leaned in. "All I know is she came with nothing. Roger asked me if my friends had any extra clothes in her size that they were getting rid of when she started staying with them. I'm not digging for details. But I think she'd really appreciate the gift card."

"It's not exactly romantic."

"It doesn't have to be the only thing you get her. And we're all getting her something." He polished off his chips as he thought about it. "Besides, supporting her dreams is romantic as hell."

Knowing what her ex had done to prevent those dreams, he nodded. "Alright, let's stop there first."

Once they cleaned up their table, Nadia showed him where the store was on the map. He'd never given much thought to where medical professionals bought their uniforms. Nadia's friend being a nurse, of course, she had.

The insane number of prints in the store overwhelmed him. "I only ever see nurses wearing plain scrubs," he said to Nadia with a scratch of his head.

"It depends on where you work. Rosie works in a children's unit, so they're allowed to wear whatever they want. Most hospitals require their people to wear specific colors to denote their role or area." She shrugged. "That's why I suggested the gift card, since she doesn't know where she'll end up yet."

He nodded. It was perfect. But it didn't give her much to unwrap. He wandered to the far back wall. Badge holders, lanyards, stethoscopes... "I thought the hospitals would provide them stethoscopes."

"Sometimes they do, and sometimes they want their own to prevent cross contamination. It's critical in a setting like a hospital." The salesperson emerged from the back door, where they probably had storage. "Can I help you find anything?" he asked.

"We're shopping for my brother's girlfriend. She's studying to be a nurse," Nadia chimed in.

A small smile lifted the corner of Finn's mouth as a sense of rightness filled his chest. Maybe his baby sister was more in tune with him than he thought.

"Okay. A gift card is always good."

"That's what I suggested."

"Yeah, but I want something bigger for under the tree." Finn interjected. The sales guy gestured at the wall of accessories.

"Then I would definitely suggest a stethoscope or some of our accessories. You can box the card with them."

Finn nodded as he moved down the wall. He still didn't know Josie's favorite color, so he didn't want to pick a stethoscope. Then his eyes snagged on something.

"What makes this a nurse's watch? Wouldn't any watch work?"

"Well, not all watches have the second hand, and this one is painted red, so it's easier to read. And those numbers around the hours? Those make it easier to take someone's pulse quickly."

Finn eyed the white nylon band and the silver casing. She could wear it anywhere. "Perfect. I'll take this and a gift card."

"Do you want a gift receipt?"

"Yeah, just in case."

"Trust me, they're very popular. I doubt she'll bring it back." He rang Finn's purchase up at the register. "And how much did you want on the gift card?"

"Nadia, how much does Rosie drop when she comes in here?"

Nadia walked up to them, a bright green stethoscope in her hand. She named a number range. "She drops that much, easy. But she buys the novelty scrubs since she can."

He didn't want Josie to have to worry at all when she got a job. And she would need a whole wardrobe of scrubs, and probably a pair of the nursing shoes he'd seen along the far wall. "Double what she said."

Nadia paid for her purchase after he charged his card and whistled at him when they left the store. "Big spender."

He felt his cheeks heat up. "It's just a gift card."

"No, Finn. It's a whole new life for her. That's shoes and enough scrubs to get through a week of shifts, no matter where she ends up. And the watch is close enough to jewelry but still super practical." She patted him on the shoulder. "She's going to love it."

BY THE TIME FINN got home, Josie was a bundle of nerves. She didn't have any more sexy nightgowns, but it dawned on her she hadn't been fully naked with Finn yet. Now that it was her choice, she wanted it. Wanted him to see her.

She rubbed at herself over her underwear, hoping to relieve some of the pressure before he got home. Images of what they'd already done together flowed through her mind. Why hadn't she done this before? No, that was silly. She knew why she'd never touched herself. First, her libido had been dormant while in captivity. Before that, Brad had been downright possessive of her, wanting to be the only one to touch her. And back home, well... masturbation was a sin.

Josie fought against her inner programming, wanting to slip beneath her panties and see how wet she was thinking of Finn.

And just like that, Finn was in her room, leaning on the doorway to the bathroom, his jaw hanging open.

"Were you missing me?"

"Yes," she whined. "So mean of you to make me think about it all day."

"Let me make it up to you, baby." He slid onto her bed and leaned his back against the footboard. "Can I watch first?"

"You want to watch me... do that?"

"I want to see what you like."

She snorted. "I don't even know."

He groaned and grasped his bulge through his jeans. "Fuck, so hot. Do it. Let me watch you explore."

An odd mixture of nerves and excitement shot through her spine. "Tell me what to do?" she whispered.

"Pull your leggings down. Take them off." Following his sultry suggestion, she tossed the leggings on the floor. His gaze was on her, flitting between her face and her pussy, his tone seductive and coaxing. "Slide your hand up under your shirt for me. That's good. Play with your nipple, now. Pinch it, roll it, see what feels good."

She rolled her tight bud between her fingers and whimpered as the sensation shot straight to her clit. Then she pinched it and gasped.

"Feel good, baby?"

"So good," she groaned. "Now what?"

"Your panties are so wet. I can see the dark spot." He massaged his dick through his pants, and she wondered if she could make him come like this. She wanted to know what it looked like, how he liked to be touched.

"Push your panties to the side and stroke your lips now. Gently." She shuddered as her fingers collected the moisture leaking from her opening. "Now run that wetness around your clit."

She moaned as she did as he said, driving her desire up and up. "I want to see you, too."

He groaned and pulled his pants down to release his cock. "As you wish." It stood straight to the sky, long and thick. Her mouth watered. She'd used to love blow jobs, one of the few things Brad allowed that made her feel powerful.

"Don't look at me like that, sweetheart, or this will be over before it's begun."

"Can't help it." She rubbed faster, putting her whole body into it. Tired of her underwear being in the way, she ripped them down and tossed them to the floor, spreading her legs wide for him to see everything.

"Look at that sopping wet pussy. Is all that for me, Sunshine?"

"Yes," she panted. "I'm so close."

"Come for me, baby, then I'm going to bury my face between those legs and eat you until I pass out."

She came with a cry and his name on her lips, and slumped against the headboard. Finn lay down next to her and waved her up.

"Do you care if I jerk myself off while you sit on my face?"

She pouted. "Yes, in fact I do." Rising to her knees, she pulled her sweater and bra off and tossed them on the floor. Finn made a choking sound.

"Josie, you don't have to…"

"I'm not doing anything I don't want to, ever again. Got me?" Finn nodded. "Now get naked."

He shucked his clothes faster than she thought possible, and she drank in all his smooth skin. He was tan to just below his waist, where his paler complexion took over. She watched as his hand moved slowly up and down his shaft, a small bead of pre-come forming at the tip.

She'd done that. Pride filled her chest.

"If you want me to sit on your face, I'm going to return the favor."

His green eyes widened, and she swore his dick got bigger somehow.

"Hop on, Sunshine."

She lifted her knee and placed her pussy inches from his mouth.

"Sit, not hover, Josie." His hand grasped her hip and pulled her down. Then his tongue was on her, lapping at her, his mouth sucking at her labia and oh God! He pointed his tongue and slid it in and out of her pussy.

Moaning, she rocked back and forth, overcome by sensation as he sucked her clit into his mouth. His hand left her hip and slid down to her entrance.

He took his mouth off her clit for a moment and circled her entrance. "Is this okay?"

"Yes! Please!" He slid a finger inside her and pumped into her while his tongue flicked at her clit. She fell forward and grasped his cock with her hand, bringing it to her mouth.

He groaned against her and slid another finger in. "God, that feels good, baby. I'm not going to last long."

She took her mouth off him long enough to say, "You can come in my mouth," and smile at his answering moan. Dipping her head once more, she swirled her tongue around the head and hollowed her cheeks as she sucked him.

His hand moved faster, like he'd lost control, and Josie grinned internally that she'd done that, too. He was long, thick, and smooth. She'd never thought of a cock as pretty, but he definitely fit the bill. Although he might not appreciate it if she said it out loud.

He crooked his fingers and hit a spot inside of her that made her hips buck harder. Then he pressed on that spot continuously, and her desire drove up and up and up, until she peaked, screaming around his dick in her mouth.

His answering groan was all the warning she got before he was spilling into her mouth, salty and sweet. She gulped down his release and cleaned his softening cock with gentle licks of her tongue, as he brought her down from her own climax.

"Fuck, Josie. That mouth is amazing."

She rolled off him to lay beside him with her head at his knees. "So is yours."

He reached down and held out his hand to help her twist around and snuggle into his arms. She winced as her hair caught under his arm.

"Did I hurt you?"

"Nope. Just my hair." She pulled it out from where it was trapped and flipped it behind her. "Your aunt is coming over tomorrow to take care of it."

"Your hair is beautiful. She'll be thrilled." Roger had explained their Aunt Louise had her own salon and had been doing the family's hair their whole lives. She always shut down for Christmas Eve, so he'd called on Josie's behalf to see if she was free for a house call.

"I'm just tired of it tangling so much. I miss having short hair."

"It's like corn silk. So pale and soft." He sifted it through his fingers.

"What did you and Nadia do?"

She felt him grin against her forehead. "She took me for my new arm."

That broke through her sated haze. "New arm?"

His voice sounded like he was going to cry. "She and her friends put together a fundraiser to get me a bionic arm. I've got a loaner right now so I can get used to the controls while they make mine."

"That's incredible! I can't wait to see it."

"Tomorrow?" he asked, his face all soft and sleepy. "It's late and I'm comfortable."

She yawned and laid back down. "I can wait."

Chapter 22

FINN SPENT CHRISTMAS EVE wrapping gifts and playing video games with Roger using his new arm. He showed it off that morning at breakfast and programmed the light to slowly shift between red and green. Aunt Louise showed up around ten and whisked Josie away to the bathroom. When they came down two hours later, Aunt Louise had a bag of Josie's hair, and Josie had the biggest smile on her face. A chin-length bob with a wispy fringe had her looking energized, and her hair looked so much healthier.

"Why'd you save the hair, Aunt Louise?" he asked.

Louise smiled at Josie. "She had just enough to donate to the kids' wigs charity. Anyway, I have to run. The grandkids are getting bikes this year and we're all putting them together. Merry Christmas everyone!"

After she'd gone, Josie turned to him. "What do you think?"

"You look amazing. With any hair." He let the ends of her hair flow through his fingers. "But the smile on your face tells me you're happy, and that's all that matters."

Pink tinged her cheeks, and she ducked her head. He lifted her chin, unaware that Roger and Jenna had come back to the kitchen. "I'm serious. You're beautiful, inside and out, Sunshine." He took her lips slowly, sipping as he pulled her into his embrace so fluidly, it was as though he had his old arm back.

He'd nearly said the L word to her last night, and it was on the tip of his tongue even now. But he didn't want her to run.

A whistle cut through the air, and they broke apart.

"I knew something was up!" crowed Jenna.

Roger just shook his head. "We both wondered."

Finn shrugged and pressed Josie closer. "Can you blame me?"

"Hell, no." Jenna made her way to the counter where the butter lay out. "Are we still baking, or did you two want to go upstairs and put something else in the oven?"

"Jenna!" cried Josie. "We talked about this."

"Yes, I know, the 'man ban'." Jenna put air quotes around the last two words. "But damn it, Josie, you deserve it."

His sunshine blushed and tucked some hair behind her ear. "Well, I wanted to get my job first and all…"

"I'm not going to stand in your way, Sunshine." He pressed his lips to her forehead. "I just want to stand next to you while you get there."

She turned her face up to him, tears gathering in her eyes. "Really?"

"Really." He kissed her again.

"Are you helping me bake this time, Josie?"

Josie sniffed. "Yes." She crossed her arms and popped a hip out. "If I leave you to bake by yourself, we won't have cookies. We'll have hockey pucks."

Jenna cackled. "Right you are. Thank God someone knows what they're doing in the kitchen around here."

"Hey!" Finn cried in fake indignation. "That's the last time I make dinner for you!"

"Sorry, sorry. Okay, two of you know your way around the kitchen. You can stay and teach me and Roger." Jenna dug out the mixing bowl he hadn't realized Roger owned and pointed at a recipe she'd printed off the internet. "Let's get cracking."

By the time they were done, flour had been smudged just about everywhere. He couldn't step anywhere in the kitchen without getting sprinkles in between his toes, but they'd had more fun than he could remember. Naturally, Josie's cookies were the best-looking, and she personally fed him one when his hand was too covered in frosting to take it from her.

Just as they finally got the kitchen cleaned back up and settled down for a Christmas movie, Roger's phone rang.

"Hey, Sam! What's your ETA?" He was silent as he listened to his friend on the other end. "That sucks, man. Where did you pull over?"

He put the phone on speaker while he searched for something on his phone.

"We're on I-70 by the Mount Airy exit. I talked to the roadside assistance, but they can't get anyone out here for at least three hours."

"Shit, man, I can come jump you and be home before they would get to you."

"If you want to, sure. I just wanted to let you know we would be heading straight to the apartment."

Right, Roger had said his friends would be coming back tonight and stopping over since it had been almost a month since they'd seen them.

A month. Damn, how time flies.

Jenna looked worried. "Are Sam and Frankie okay?"

"My battery died, Jenna, no big deal." Sam said through the phone. "Someone's a little hangry, but I think we'll survive."

"I'll be there in about an hour, Sam. Stay warm."

"Will do. See you soon."

Jenna rose with Roger. "I want to come, too. I miss Frankie."

"I don't know if that's a good idea." Roger's gaze flicked to Josie, then back to Jenna. Finn couldn't see Jenna's face from where he sat, but he hoped she was trying to convince Roger to give them alone time.

He cleared his throat. "I can protect her."

Roger nodded. "You know where my safe is."

"And the code, unless you've changed it."

"Nope." Roger tied his boots and slipped his coat on. "I'll get alerted if there's any kind of security breach. And I'll call you immediately."

Finn gave him a two-fingered salute with the bionic arm. "You got it."

Roger and Jenna bundled up against the Christmas Eve chill and locked the door behind them.

"Are we still going to watch the movie?" Josie asked.

He slung his arm over her shoulder and she snuggled into him. "Yeah, Sunshine. Hit play." The classic story about a boy who just wanted a BB gun for Christmas always made him laugh. Maybe it was because he'd been on the rifle team, or maybe it was the scene where he got his tongue stuck to the telephone pole.

When the credits rolled, Josie turned to him. "That's… different from the other Christmas movies I've been watching with Jenna."

"Yeah, it is. It's a bit more realistic, to be honest." He leaned forward to turn the movie off. "What did you think?"

Her eyebrows drew down as she thought about it. "I think I like the other ones better."

"Really? What was your favorite Christmas present when you were a kid?"

She blushed a deep scarlet and turned away. "My parents didn't do Christmas."

"What?" Had he heard her correctly?

"My parents didn't do Christmas. Or any holiday, really." She turned to face him. "Their church forbade it. So I had to sit in school and listen to all the kids talking about it. Any holiday-themed crafts my class did, I had to be excused and go sit by myself in the conference room. But during recess and lunch, they'd talk about what they were going to ask Santa for. After we got back from winter break, they'd all brag about what they got. I was the only one who didn't get anything."

She wiped at a tear that had escaped and huffed a fake laugh. "Sorry. I didn't mean to dump all that on you. I'm only learning now how much I missed out on. Maybe it's because it's all new to me, but I like the movies with the magic better."

As she spoke, a knot formed in Finn's stomach. How had he missed this? No wonder she'd been overwhelmed by the holiday outlet. "That makes perfect sense. In fact..." He snatched the Santa hat with the attached beard that Jenna had bought as a joke for Roger, sliding it on his head and fixing the mouth hole over his lips. "Why don't you sit on Santa's lap now?"

She giggled as he helped her slide onto his lap, doing his best "ho, ho, ho." "Now, Miss Josie, you've been extremely good, and it appears I missed your house for a long time. So you can ask for as many Christmas wishes as you want."

Josie clapped a hand over her giggling mouth, then took a deep breath and pressed further into him. She played with the fake beard as she responded. "Gee, Santa, I can really only think of one thing I want. He's handsome, and he's funny once you get to know him. I love how patient and kind he is, and that he cooks for me. Unfortunately, he thinks he's not worthy because he lost an arm in combat.

But I think he's a hero and I..." Her gray eyes stared down into his as his pulse raced. Soft fingers dropped to play with the neckline of his t-shirt, sending electric tingles across his skin. "Do you think that's possible?"

Finn's heart beat like the little drummer boy as he ripped the beard and hat from his head. She saw him, all of him. God, he loved her. Even if she wasn't there yet, he'd wait. He pushed through the thickening in his throat and croaked out, "I'm yours, baby. I'm all yours."

SHE CRASHED HER MOUTH to his, cupping his precious face in her hands. Her stomach fluttered and her pussy wept as she turned to straddle his hips. She rocked back and forth over the bulge in his pants, and his hands clenched into fists at his side.

No, that wouldn't do. Her skin cried out for his touch. She needed to be filled, and she wouldn't be satisfied with grinding this time. She wanted all of him.

"You're not touching me."

Finn groaned. "I want... Everything has to be your idea. You're leading this. I won't pressure you."

"You're not like them, Finn. I know the difference."

He bit his lip, his jaw clenched. She picked up his left hand and slid it up under her sweatshirt, over her breast. After that, she reached behind and unhooked her bra.

His Adam's apple bobbed as he swallowed. "You're sure?"

Maybe her Marine needed a dose of his own medicine. Josie's cheeks heated as she said the words but forced them out despite her blood pounding in her ears. "I need it, Finn. I need y-your hard cock in my p-pussy. I need you to... to cover up everyone else who was there first. Erase them. *Please.*"

He got even harder beneath her, and she moaned.

"Fuck me, Finn!" Before she started crying. She hadn't realized why she needed this so badly until the words poured from her soul.

His sharp inhale was the only clue she'd broken through his control. "Not here." He wrapped his left arm around her back and stood up, making her cling to his shoulders. "Hold on tight." Finn jogged up the stairs, every step driving her arousal higher as she rubbed against him. By the time he got to his bedroom, she was panting for him. As she started to rip her sweatshirt over her head, his hands stilled hers. "Let me." He stood over where she lay on his bed, looking at her like she was magical.

Deft hands removed her clothing until she lay in nothing but her soaked panties. He held himself up on one arm over her. "I can't put my weight on this one."

"Lay down, then." They switched places, and Josie took her place on top once more. "I'm going to unwrap my present a little early." She put a finger to her lips.

"I won't tell Santa." Finn grinned. He popped his arm off and laid it on the nightstand. She rolled his shirt up and over his head while he sat up. Josie ran her fingers over his skin, leaning over to follow her fingers with her mouth. Licking, sucking, running her tongue over his nipples until his chest heaved beneath her and a small wet spot appeared on his pants. Although, to be fair, that could be from her. But it didn't matter.

She took her time sliding down his body, pulling his pants over his impressive cock and sliding them off. "No underwear?"

"I was in a rush."

"A likely story." She licked a line up the underside of his dick and suppressed her giggle at the whine that came from his throat.

"Josie, I'm on edge here. If you want me in that pussy, you better hurry up."

With a jolt, she realized she'd forgotten protection. "Um, condom?"

"Check the drawer." He pointed at the nightstand. Reluctantly, she rose and slid it open. There sat an unopened box of "ribbed for her pleasure" condoms.

She slid her nail across the seal, popped the box open, and took out a foil packet. "I appreciate that you're prepared."

Finn chuckled. "I made the offer. Wanted to have them on hand in case you took me up on it."

She slid the rubber down his shaft and dropped her panties to the floor. Pressing both hands into his chest, she threw one leg over him, but leaned down to kiss him. He kissed her back like a man starved, his elbow reaching up for her as his left thumb rubbed her nipple.

With a cry, she broke the kiss, and leaned back to finally, finally slide him inside. But then she had an idea. She didn't want to be doing all the work here. "Sit up against the headboard," she told him, and he scrambled to comply. She had to crawl forward again to achieve what she wanted, but after she was sliding into his lap, slowly stretching herself around his cock. It had been months since she'd had anything inside her, and years since she'd enjoyed sex at all. And he wasn't small by any stretch of the imagination. Sheathing him inside with her legs wrapped around his hips blew her mind. It felt so good.

Because it was *Finn*.

While she tried to catch her breath, Finn pulled his knees up, supporting her back. She leaned her forehead against his.

God, it was so hard not to say "I love you." But it was too soon. So Josie kissed him again, arching her back so he could lave kisses down her neck and to her breasts, sucking first one nipple and then the other.

"Move when you're ready." Sweat beaded on his brow, and she knew he was as affected as she was. Laying her arms over his shoulders for leverage, she ground her clit against his pubic bone, then rose up on her knees and slid back down. Slowly at first, until she got her rhythm. Faster, harder. God, he was so deep inside her!

When Finn planted his feet and started thrusting beneath her, he hit that spot inside and she saw stars. She cried out and dug her nails into his back as they came together, over and over, harder, and harder. "Come for me, Josie!"

Yes! Her vision went white, and she screamed her climax, vaguely aware of Finn's shout half a second behind her. He thrust a few more times, drawing out their orgasms. When she blinked her eyes open once more, she was leaning back against his legs, and he had thrown his head back against the headboard. Both of them panted like they'd run a marathon.

Leaning forward, she pressed a kiss to his throat. "Best Christmas ever."

He grinned and grasped the edge of the condom as he softened inside her. "Good. Hop off and I'll take care of this."

She scoffed. "I am not hopping anywhere, anytime soon." She rolled off his dick and fell into the mattress. He chuckled, stood on shaky legs, and headed for the bathroom.

He returned quickly and leaned over to kiss her. "Do you want to shower with me?"

"Is there enough room?"

"It'll have to be a friendly shower." His serious look disintegrated when he waggled his eyebrows at her. "Come on, Sunshine."

She took his hand and followed him into the bathroom, where he already had the water heating. Her brain must not have come back online yet because she asked a question before she thought about it. "Do you call me that because of my hair?"

He turned and gave her a rueful smile. "Not entirely." Gesturing for her to enter the shower first, he followed behind and slid the glass door shut.

Steam quickly filled the cube as she poured some body wash into her loofah. "Why then?"

"Because I was stuck in the darkness. Literally. Just ask Roger how he found me at my parents' house." She snorted a laugh, and he smiled. "Anyway, I was stuck in the darkness, and then I get here, and you were like a ray of sunshine. Which, given your history, is even more incredible than I originally thought." He pumped shampoo from the pump bottle one handed and began to wash her hair. She hummed as she leaned back against him, letting him pamper her. "You're incredible."

She kissed him, turned, and leaned back to rinse out her hair. His eyes dropped to the water sluicing over her breasts. She took her loofah and put his body wash in it. "Your turn."

Chapter 23

CHRISTMAS DAY DAWNED BRIGHT and clear. Roger and Jenna must have come in after she and Finn had fallen asleep. The scent of coffee drifted up the stairs, and Josie's eyes popped open. She'd never truly understood the phrase, "like a kid on Christmas" until that morning.

Before she could escape the sheets, Finn's hand clamped over her breast and he pulled her in tighter. "Mmm," he murmured, nobbling her ear. "There's a naked girl in my bed. I must have been a very good boy."

"Or a bad one," she taunted. They'd fallen asleep before they had a chance to put pajamas on, and she was suddenly hyper aware of the hard cock that was rubbing between her legs, soaking itself in her juices.

Finn's hand tweaked her nipple, and she shuddered. Just like that, her mind went to one thing and one thing alone. "Can you ... do it like this?"

"Mmm, fuck you?"

"Y-yes." That F word was still hard to say.

"No, baby. I'm going to make love to you like this."

That made her melt into the mattress. His hand disappeared, and she heard the rip of a foil packet, then his muffled curse as he got it over himself one-handed. When his heat was at her back once more, his hand slipped between her thighs and pulled one leg up and backward over his. "Let's see if you're ready for me."

He slipped his fingers through her honey and she moaned. "Such a needy pussy. I'm going to take such good care of you." He drew his hand up back to his mouth, and she heard him smack his lips. "So tasty."

"Please!" Her whisper came out hoarse, need pulsing through her. He slid right inside, and she panted as he turned her head and kissed her lips.

"Touch your nipples for me, baby. I'll need my hand to hold you steady."

She complied with a whine, cupping her breasts while he grasped her hip and thrust away. His mouth attached to her neck with a sucking kiss, and she writhed in his embrace.

He was hitting her G-spot every time he thrust inside at this angle. Josie spiraled higher, higher, higher than she'd ever gone. Then his fingers drifted over her hip to her clit and rolled over it. She cried out as her walls spasmed around his thick shaft, her orgasm crashing into her.

"Fuck! Josie!" Finn's thrusts became erratic, spasmodic. He thrust one last time as deep as he could, setting her off again while her pussy twitched with the aftershocks.

They came down together, panting; him clutching her to him like a lifeline. Josie bit her tongue to keep the confessions of love inside that threatened to spill from her lips. She would not tie herself to a man when she couldn't stand on her own two feet. He said he was hers, and sure she was his, but part of her refused to cross that line officially until she was ready. As it was, if he left her, her heart would never recover.

But it didn't seem like he was on the same page. He nuzzled her ear. "Josie, I... I just have to say..." She stiffened in his embrace. If he said it, she didn't know what she'd do. Then he whispered in her ear. "Merry Christmas."

She relaxed with a sigh. "Merry Christmas, indeed." He pulled away, probably to take care of the condom. Stumbling from the bed, she waited outside the bathroom door until he emerged. "All yours," he said. "I'm going to get dressed and go downstairs. Take your time."

"Are you kidding? It's Christmas!"

He laughed as she shut the door. "Alright, I'll see you down there. If I wait for you, it's going to be dinnertime before we get out of this room."

She cupped her face as she felt it heat up. "My clothes are in my room, anyway. So, yeah."

"I'll go make sure Jenna doesn't burn the cinnamon rolls."

JOSIE RAN DOWN THE stairs like her butt was on fire just as Jenna pulled the rolls out of the oven.

"Those smell amazing."

"Merry Christmas!" Jenna shouted. "Sounds like you two got the celebrations started without us."

"I didn't think you'd want to join in," Finn deadpanned. Josie felt her cheeks turning red.

"I was excited, and I unwrapped one of my presents early."

Jenna snickered as she smothered the cinnamon rolls in the glaze. "Get it, girl!"

Josie laughed as the embarrassment faded. "What happened with Sam and Frankie?" It had been a month since she'd seen the quiet, unassuming computer guy and his outspoken girlfriend.

"We got them jumped, followed them to the apartment, and helped them unload the truck and the trailer. Then they crashed, and we came home. But they're fine."

"They'll be at Mom and Dad's today for dinner." Roger waved from where he sat at the island. He finished his cup of coffee and went for another. "Anyone else want some?"

"Sure," Josie said with a yawn.

Roger smirked at his brother. "You could have let her sleep more last night."

"I'm excited about my first Christmas." Josie defended him, though he wore a smug grin. She leaned over to whisper in his ear. "I won't complain about a little lost sleep."

"Me neither." He kissed her softly on the lips, pulling out a chair for her. "Those rolls should be cool enough to plate now, Jenna."

Soon, they all had warm rolls and coffee in front of them. Josie moaned around the bite in her mouth. "Is this another family tradition?"

Jenna shrugged. "It's one of mine. The cook always made them for breakfast on Christmas morning. These are just out of a can, but at least they're edible."

"I can bake cookies from scratch, but breads? Forget it. Besides, these are delicious."

Jenna lit the tree using her phone and wiped her hands on a napkin. "Come on, there are presents to open!"

Oh no. Josie realized with a sinking feeling in her gut that she hadn't been able to shop for anyone.

"What's that look for, Sunshine?" Finn asked, leaving the last bite of his breakfast on the plate.

"I didn't get anything for anyone else. I don't have any money of my own..." Her voice trailed off as she bit her lip.

Finn cupped her face and angled it back toward him. "Everyone understands, sweetheart. We're just grateful you're here with us. Especially me." He wrapped his arms around her—when had he put the prosthetic on?—and hugged her tight. Dropping his mouth to her ear, he whispered, "You're the best Christmas present, Sunshine."

"So are you." Her eyes watered, and she blinked the tears back. No crying on Christmas.

He took her hand, and they followed Jenna and Roger into the living room, where Jenna was already rummaging through the brightly wrapped boxes under the tree. Roger sat on the couch looking at her with a faraway look on his face, like he couldn't believe how lucky he'd gotten.

Josie couldn't believe how lucky she'd gotten, either. Jenna and Frankie had masterminded her rescue. If it weren't for them... she didn't want to think about it.

The redheaded elf popped up and handed Josie a box wrapped in reindeer paper. "This one's for you."

Josie read the tag. "To Josie, From Jenna and Roger." Before she could contemplate the wonder of her first Christmas present, she yelped as she was yanked backward. Finn had taken the recliner and pulled her to sit on his lap.

Once situated there, she slid her thumb under the flap of paper, trying not to tear it.

"Aw, come on! Rip into it! That's half the fun!" Jenna egged her on from her spot on the floor. Josie looked at Roger, then at Finn.

"Open it however you want to," Finn reassured her.

She pulled, and the paper gave a very satisfying sound. Maybe she wasn't as violent as Jenna was trying to get her to be with it, but ripping made it go faster.

When the paper fell away, a white box was left behind. Josie lifted the lid, and her jaw dropped open. "I love it!" She lifted it up to get a better look. They'd bought her a sweatshirt that said "Cool Nurse's Club" in multicolored letters on a cream-colored background. It might wash her out, but who cared? She grinned and hugged it. "Thank you!"

"You're welcome!" Jenna grinned.

"Jenna, can you get that one with the gold paper and hand it to Josie for me?" asked Finn. "Thanks."

Josie laid the sweatshirt down on the coffee table and took the small shiny package from Jenna. Long and thin, what could it be?

She smiled at the tag. It read, "To my sunshine, from Finn."

Her heart melted. She pulled the paper off and out slid a clear plastic box with a white watch inside.

"Nurse's watch?" She read it out loud and looked at the back. "Red second hand makes taking a pulse easier, and the extra numbers on the outside correspond to seconds so you can add up quickly. Water resistant." Her words failed her as her jaw dropped open and she blinked back tears of joy. He'd meant what he said about supporting her.

Brad had claimed he supported her dreams, but when push came to shove, he fought against her every step of the way. Finn was not only giving her the words, but he had just given her tangible proof he wanted her to succeed.

But that wasn't even the main gift. "Keep going." Reaching back into the paper, she pulled out a gift card for a scrub store. "Nadia said her friend goes there for her scrubs and shoes. I got the gift card, so when you get that job, you won't have to worry about buying your uniform, whatever color it has to be."

"Nurses have to buy their own uniforms?" Roger's voice was indignant.

"That's what Nad said. And given how many scrubs this place had, it's pretty normal."

Josie could barely make out the number on the card through her tears. "That's... Finn, that's too much!"

"No, it's not. I don't want you to have to worry about a thing except your boards, okay?" His hand rubbed circles on her back as she turned and slumped against him, clutching his precious gift.

"Josie, you okay?" Crap, now Jenna was worried about her.

She sniffed and wiped her eyes with the tissue Roger held out. "I'm fine. I'm just... overwhelmed."

"Well, I think you're done until we get to my parents' house." Finn held her close.

"I didn't get anything for anyone else!"

"Would you feel better if I put your name on the tags?"

"No." She pouted. "I'll have a job by next year. Right?" She looked over at Roger. "You would have a better idea how these things go than me."

Roger just shook his head. "Not really. I sent a message to Ross the other day, and he said stand by. So hopefully soon."

Finn pressed his lips to her forehead. "Do you want to stay down here for the rest of it?"

"Yes."

"Alright. Jenna, grab the green box down there and hand it to your worse half, please."

"MERRY CHRISTMAS!" MOM GREETED them at the door, taking their coats and hats. She hugged each of them, including Josie, which made Finn's heart warm. She looked at the two of them standing together and grinned. Finn put a finger to his lips and lifted his eyebrow. *Keep quiet, Mom*, he begged.

Mom took the hint and ushered them into the living room. Their stockings, embroidered with their names that they'd used since childhood, hung over the fireplace. Finn grinned when he saw that Mom had added to the collection. Last year, Caleb's stocking had hung next to Nadia's. This year, Jenna, Sam, Frankie, and Josie had all been added to the lineup.

"You've been busy, Mom." He leaned over and kissed her on the cheek. "They look great."

Judy beamed. "Well, after all, it's Christmas." Josie wandered toward the tree, Jenna in tow. Finn waved his mom into the kitchen.

She followed with a confused look on her face. "Finn, what's going on? Are you and Josie...?"

He sighed. "It's new, and she's skittish. She's had a rough time and we're going slow. But that's not what I wanted to tell you." He took a deep breath. Mom would understand. "She got overwhelmed with the gifts this morning, and she only opened two. So if there are any tears, don't say anything, okay? She seemed embarrassed about it."

Mom nodded. "Okay, thanks for the warning. We weren't sure what to get her. Nadia has a small thing for her, and your father and I just got her a gift card she can use for whatever."

"It'll be fine. She also felt bad she doesn't have gifts for anyone."

"We've all been there." Mom patted his arm. "Will you help me lift the turkey while you're in here? Oh, wait." She palmed her face. "I'm not thinking. Send Roger in, would you? I just need to check the bird."

He grinned. "I can do it now." He lifted his right arm, demonstrating the bionic hand. "Nadia gave me my present early."

Mom's gasp drew a crowd. "Finn, that's incredible!"

"I know. Now let me at that roasting pan."

Chapter 24

THE DAY AFTER CHRISTMAS, he used his new membership to the gun range. Roger had purchased him an annual plan to the same place the rifle team practiced at. They even had a selection of rifles to rent, including the M40 he'd trained on when he first joined the Marines. Later, he'd switched to the Mk 13, which the range didn't have, but the M40 would do.

At some point, he'd want to buy his own. But for now, he was too eager to get back on the range and test his new arm to wait.

He showed his license at the desk and paid for his ammunition, paper targets, and a half-hour rental. The guy behind the desk gave him his lane number and ear protectors, then Finn strode back to lane twenty-three.

After he set up his target, Finn settled the familiar weight in his arms. He lined up the sights with the center of the bull's eye, released a breath, and squeezed the trigger. The recoil startled him. He'd forgotten how the older model jumped more. Shaking his shoulders and rolling his neck, he lifted the rifle again and fired.

When the magazine had emptied, Finn retrieved his target. His spread was wider than he remembered from his last practice session, but of course he was dealing with a bionic hand that didn't respond as quickly as his original one. If he had been aiming at a moving target, he'd need to adjust his timing. He pinned up a new target and sent it back. Reloading, he went through another magazine.

As he reviewed his second target, someone tapped on his shoulder. Finn jumped, spinning around to see Coach Atkins grinning at him. He removed his earmuffs and shook the old man's hand. "Hey, Coach."

"You playing with a new toy?"

Finn held up the new arm. "I am."

"Nice! Is that like Timmy's?"

He shrugged. "I don't know if it's the same company, but it's bionic. Apparently my little sister had a fundraising campaign already in motion and I had no idea."

"No shit?"

"No, sir. She surprised me a few days ago. Technically this is the loaner while they make mine. I'm getting used to the controls and the app that goes with it."

That reminded him of the software in the arm. He'd see if he could adjust the response time.

"That's amazing. Hey, while I have you here, I want to ask you something."

"What's that?"

"I'm looking for an assistant coach. It's a volunteer gig, but the kids really liked talking to you at practice."

"I'll have to see. My brother wanted me to come work for him, so I'll talk to him about it. But I'll let you know."

"Great! Have fun with the new arm." He patted Finn on the shoulder and walked over to his own lane.

Finn looked at the paper target with fresh determination. Then he pinned up a fresh target and kept going.

He might not be Eagle Eye anymore, but he was back.

THE FRONT DOOR SLAMMED shut, bringing Josie out of her study haze. She could practically recite the words of the guide in her sleep at this point. But the desire to pass was nearly as strong as her desire for Finn.

She stood when he came into the living room. "Hey, Sunshine." He kicked off his shoes and greeted her with a kiss.

"How did it go?" Josie asked, despite the glow in his face giving the answer away.

"Amazing. The response time is a little slow, but I think I can tweak that in the app."

"I'm so happy for you." She cupped his face and kissed him again.

"I need to talk to Roger, but hopefully, this will mean I can take care of your protection officially." He pressed his forehead to hers. "I know it's probably too soon, and I understand if you can't say it back, but I have to. Josie, I l-"

"Josie! You have a phone call!" Roger called from the office. He came running into the living room, his phone in his hand. Since Frankie, Sam and Ross had felt it would be safer to not give her a phone yet, all calls came through Roger's phone. But there was only one person who could be calling.

Roger laid the phone down on the coffee table as he sat on the armchair, ignoring the glare emanating from his brother. "I've got you on speaker, Ross."

"Merry Christmas, Hunt Security! Josie, how are you?"

"I-I'm fine." She sank down onto the couch in a daze. Agent Patterson had awful timing. She was 99 percent certain Finn had just been about to tell her he loved her, and she wasn't sure how to feel right now.

"I'm glad. I've got good news and bad news. We've finally managed to get a lead to the syndicate with an undercover agent in Baltimore. The plan is to use a sting operation. We're sending in a woman that's been outfitted with a wire, and a GPS tracker, to be taken hostage so we can locate them and collect evidence at the same time."

"Sounds solid," Roger interjected.

"You haven't heard the bad news yet." Ross sighed. "They know Josie's alive."

"H-how?" Her heart thumped against her chest as Finn clenched his fist. Even though she'd known it would be unlikely, she realized a secret part of her had hoped the syndicate hadn't missed her.

"My insider isn't sure. He's not fully trusted yet, so they're not very forthcoming. He overheard your name and managed to pry it out of his contact."

Roger scrubbed a hand over his face. "What now?"

"My supervisors want me to ask if you'd do it."

Finn growled and Roger shook his head. "Ross, you can't be serious! They have to know she talked to the authorities. She might not make it to the holding tank alive."

"I want to do it."

"Josie?" Finn stared down at her with alarm before perching on the sofa next to her.

Ross paused in what he had planned to say. "Are you sure about that?"

She nodded, but realized he couldn't see her. "I am."

"Sunshine, it's too dangerous. They'll be mad that you got away and ... they might take it out on you." Worry creased Finn's face.

"I'm sorry. I have to." Her stomach dropped, and she tore her gaze away from him. She'd sworn she'd do whatever she could to get those captives out. The syndicate wouldn't look a gift horse in the mouth. Someone new, or someone they'd had before? It was perfect. "Getting me back would make them more likely to take the bait, right, Ross?"

"Possibly." Ross sounded cautious over the phone. "Are you absolutely sure you want to volunteer for this, Josie? Finn isn't wrong about the danger. I could send in an agent instead."

"I couldn't live with myself if I didn't do everything I could to save them. Besides, the minute your agent gets there, they'll know something is up. They'll know she's not me."

"I'll call you back once I've talked to them. Just wanted to give you an update."

"Thanks for getting back to us, Ross." Roger called into the phone. His eyes were also trained on Josie, but he was calm, whereas Finn panted beside her with heavy breaths.

"Bye for now." The call ended, and she met Roger's gaze with her own.

"You don't have to do it, Josie." Roger's voice stayed calm and steady. Josie was grateful. "You're safe, and there's no reason to put yourself in danger when they have female agents who are trained for this."

She trembled in her seat. Not from fear, just from the memories. "I've already lived it, Roger. Why should we subject an agent to it when I know what I'm getting into? And while I'm safe and sound, playing house with the sweetest man—" she patted Finn's knee "—there are people held captive that didn't get a Christmas tree. They probably barely had dinner. They're scared and tired and they don't know when the next job will be forced on them."

"Sunshine." Finn grabbed her face, holding her like she was going to disappear. "I can't lose you."

"You heard Ross. They'll have a tracker on me. I'll be fine."

Roger stood, pocketing his phone. "I'll let you know when he calls back."

Josie looked up and nodded as best she could.

"I'll meet you downstairs when you're ready, Finn." She furrowed her brow before she remembered the heavy bag in the basement as he walked back to his office.

Finn pulled her into his embrace, and Josie realized he was shaking. "Finn? Are you mad at me?"

"No. I'm angry at Ross for even thinking about this. And I'm..." He hesitated, then looked away. "I'm terrified."

"Finn, please try to understand. I need the closure. I need to fight back." Tears sprang to her eyes. He supported her career, couldn't he support her in this?

He squeezed his eyes shut even as he hugged her so tight she was practically in his lap. "If you're doing this, I'm going along."

Josie ignored the alarms in her head, telling her he'd just mess up the operation, and nodded. She'd promise him anything so she could go without a fight.

"It'll be okay," she murmured. "I promise."

He sighed. "Don't make promises you can't keep, Sunshine. I know all too well how simple things can go belly-up in an instant."

Ross called them back the next morning. "Josie, my boss agreed with you. Our agent is planting the information that he found you. He confirmed they want you alive. And he's going to set up a rendezvous. I'll be in touch again with more information. Don't make plans for a few days."

She snorted in response. "I can't exactly make plans when I'm in hiding, Ross."

"Good point. Just wanted to mention it. Once this gets rolling, it's going to happen quickly."

"I appreciate the warning."

"I'll call soon."

Finn vibrated on the couch next to her, every muscle in his body clenched tight. He'd held out hope that Ross's superior would come to their senses and veto Josie's participation. But that now lay dashed against the rocks while his nerves pounded against the shore of his sanity. Beating against the heavy bag downstairs wouldn't be enough this time.

"I'm going to the range." He rose from the couch and strode to the front door. Josie followed him.

"Finn?"

He stood up from pulling his shoes on. "I'm not mad at you, baby. I just need to shoot something." Her brows pulled down tight over her stormy gray eyes. Unable to help himself, he cupped her face and claimed her mouth, swallowing her moan. He forced himself to pull away. "I'll be back later."

This time, he rented an automatic rifle, and told the guy working the counter to start him a tab. He had no idea how long it would take for his nerves to settle.

Ratatatat! His heart beat in time with the bullets. The recoil made his shoulder ache. But he pressed on. Pain was good. It meant you were alive. And the pain in his shoulder distracted him from the fear in his heart.

He couldn't lose Josie. His world would go dark again, and this time, Finn didn't think he'd survive.

FINN GROANED ON HIS brother's couch. His arm thumped with his pulse. It had swollen so much he'd had to take the prosthesis off as soon as he got home. He still wasn't sure how he'd driven with it on. Damn, he'd been stupid.

Josie hurried in with another bag of ice. "Goodness, Finn, what did you *do*?"

"I just overdid it. I'll be fine." She handed him a glass of water and his pain pill. He lifted a tired eyebrow, giving her a look that said, "Really?"

"Roger ordered Chinese. I'll make you a plate." She gestured to the pill. "You need this."

He swallowed the pill and made to get up. "You don't have to wait on me. I can get it."

She pushed him down with more force than he expected, and his ass sank right back into the couch. "You can barely move. Don't argue with me."

He watched her ass bounce as she stomped off. And his dick stood at attention. "Yes, ma'am."

Something he'd forgotten about the sun since it was winter. It could warm you up, or it could burn you to a crisp. He scrubbed a hand through his hair as he contemplated that maybe he'd underestimated his girl.

She returned with two plates, one piled high with beef and broccoli, the other with sweet and sour chicken. "Pick one."

"Whichever one you don't want."

Josie handed him the beef and set the chicken down on the coffee table.

"Didn't you eat?"

She looked up at him through her lashes. "I was waiting for you."

Now he felt like an even bigger ass.

"I'll be right back with silverware."

"Did my brother get egg rolls?" He called out, and she returned with full hands.

"Of course he got egg rolls." She set the bag down next to their plates. "Eat up before the pain pill gives you a stomachache."

The silence while they ate pulled at Finn until he had to speak. "I'm sorry."

She finished chewing her bite and laid her fork down. "Do you understand why I need to do this?"

He licked his lips. "I'm trying, baby, I really am." Setting his egg roll down, he reached for her hand. She held it tight.

After a moment, she spoke again. "Imagine if your unit had been captured by the enemy, and you escaped. Would you be willing to let someone else go in and get them out?"

His answer flew from his lips before he had a chance to think about it. "Fuck, no." Oh. Oh shit. Damn, she was right. Josie had been caught up in a war the same as he had. Only she had no say in the matter. He leaned over and pressed a kiss to her forehead. "I understand now." But he didn't have to like it. She leaned her head against his with a sigh.

"Thank you."

"Give 'em hell, baby."

Chapter 25

Ross had been right. It only took a day for the FBI to have the set up ready to go. Three days after Ross's initial call, she, Roger, and Finn met Ross at an office just north of the city.

"Josie, Roger, nice to see you again." Ross shook their hands, tilting his head at Finn.

"Ross, this is my youngest brother, Finn."

"Nice to meet you."

Finn's scowl was back in place. "I'm Josie's boyfriend."

Josie's head snapped to look at him. That was the first she'd heard of it. He hadn't even asked her!

"Ah." Ross nodded, a knowing look in his eye. "I'm going to do my best to keep her safe, Finn." Then he turned to Josie and waved over another agent. "Josie, this is Agent Horne. She's going to set you up with that wire and tracker, okay?"

She nodded as she took in the petite blonde woman who had a few years on her.

Finn crossed his arms across his chest and scowled. "What's stopping this asshole from just shooting her to keep her quiet?"

Lord help her, but the overprotective thing was hot. Even though she could see where Nadia got her nickname for her brothers.

Ross turned back to him. "My agent has it on good authority that the orders are to take her in alive for questioning. And in this organization, people who defy orders don't survive."

"Are you sure you want to do this?" Finn dropped his arms, still clenching his hands at his sides. But he wouldn't look at her.

"You know I am."

Ross stepped forward again. "If you change your mind, you can back out, Josie. Agent Horne is prepared to take your place." The female agent gave a brisk nod. They had a similar build, but then memories of the girls that she'd suffered alongside only firmed her resolve. Why should she be the only one to escape? Why should she be the one with three meals a day and a soft bed to lay in at night?

Besides, they'd know it wasn't her when they got her to the syndicate. Agent Horne would be in danger and the whole operation would fail.

Her *boyfriend* stood next to Roger, behind Ross. They'd have to discuss this later. She let him see the determination in her face, and turned back to Ross. "I'm sure."

The female agent waved her toward the door. "Come to the ladies' room with me, and we'll get you wired."

Josie followed Agent Horne through the nondescript hallways to the women's bathroom. "How will this tracker work?"

"It's a small chip under an adhesive strip we place behind your ear. Like a bandage, but smaller."

"Okay. And it won't fall off?"

"Not for several days. But the plan is to get your location and get in the same day. You shouldn't be gone more than twelve hours."

Twelve hours was a long time for the syndicate to have her. But Josie could do it. She'd done it for six months, after all. Twelve hours compared to six months was nothing.

She pulled off her sweater and Agent Horne slid the microphone under her bra, tucking the transmitter inside the cup. She'd worn a slightly larger one than she needed as directed, just for this purpose. Stuffing the other side with toilet paper made the difference disappear. After she pulled her shirt back on, she lifted her hair so Agent Horne could place the tracker. Knowing the FBI would have her exact location in case the syndicate moved her, gave her a sense of security.

Everything was going to be fine.

Horne led her back to the conference room, where Finn was pacing. Ross and Roger chatted in low tones.

Ross turned as they entered the room. "All good?"

"She's all set, Ross," answered Agent Horne.

"Good." He waved them out. "Let's go down to the van. I'll explain on the way."

Finn attached himself to her side, clasping onto her hand with his bionic one. Thank goodness his swelling had gone down enough for him to wear it.

Ross waited until they got in the elevator to go over the plan. "Agent Lucas Graham is the one undercover on this assignment. He's going to blindfold you and take you into the meeting room and leave you there with his contact. The goal is for this contact to take you to a secondary location—" Finn clenched her hand, and she winced, slipping it out of his grip. "—with other captives. We will be tracking your location at all times. We will be listening at all times. I want you to give me a code, a word or a phrase that will tell me something's wrong, okay?"

"I have to go to church on Sunday."

Ross nodded. "Perfect. Work that in and I'll know to pull you out."

Wrapping her hand around Finn's bicep, Josie's heart pounded against her chest. Adrenaline pulsed through her veins as they piled into two unmarked vans. Ross made sure to show them the listening receivers.

"We'll be right outside listening."

Still, Josie trembled as the van drove closer to their destination. To the meetup point.

They stopped just outside an abandoned warehouse surrounded by woods. Josie exited the van with the guys and clung to Finn's arm. Ross pointed down the hill. "That's the meetup point. Graham has already confirmed his contact is here. He called from the other van on the way over."

A guy with a blonde buzz cut approached in street clothes. "Hi, Josie. I'm Agent Graham." He shook her trembling hand. "Inside, I'm Jameson, okay? That's how Rocky knows me."

She nodded.

"Our story is that I found you working in the supermarket, recognized you from the files, and followed you home after work. The syndicate member believes I've kidnapped you."

"Rude." She broke the tension. Everyone chuckled except Finn.

Lucas brought a fabric bag up. "I'm going to ask you to put this over your head for believability."

"Anything I should or shouldn't say?"

"As long as you don't use my real name or blow our cover, you're fine."

Josie nodded. This would hardly even qualify as acting. She was as frightened as a fish in a shark tank.

She took the bag from Lucas, but before she could put it on, Finn grabbed her chin and turned her head. "Sunshine..." he grated out. Pain, concern, and fear flitted across his features, but he cupped her face and slammed his mouth on hers. Josie clutched at his jacket. Their kiss was a tangle of tongues and teeth, and when he let her up for air, she knew she'd been claimed.

Still in a bit of a daze, she looked around. More agents had arrived, cars hidden in the woods.

"Backup," Lucas explained. He lifted his chin to Finn and gestured to her to follow him. "Alright, Josie. Show time." He helped her into a small red hatchback and pulled out a length of rope.

"Sorry, I have to bind your hands." Nodding, she buckled in first, and put the bag over her head. After he wrapped her hands in the rope, he slipped a finger between the rope and her skin to make sure it wouldn't be too tight.

"Patterson, can you hear me?" Lucas asked. "Okay, he gave me the thumbs up. He'll be in the van with your bodyguard and your boyfriend. I'm going to drive us down. Just remember, I'll be acting."

Josie nodded. "O-okay."

"We got you, darlin'." He patted her shoulder and shut the car door.

Finn's face came immediately to mind. "I know."

The hatchback rumbled over the gravel driveway down to the warehouse. It took all of five minutes before Agent Graham disappeared and Jameson came out.

He opened her door, and unbuckled her seat belt, then grabbed her arm and roughly pulled her out of the car.

"Let's go!"

"Where are we?" She made a show of it, pulling back and trying to get away. He pulled her back and marched her into the musty, echoing warehouse.

"Yo, Jameson!" came a familiar voice.

Her spine went ramrod straight. No, it couldn't be?

"Hey, Rocky. You got the money?"

"I don't get paid until I deliver her. Don't worry, man, you'll get your cut."

Lucas pulled her closer, keeping her away from that unsettling voice. "I get my cut now, or I'll take her myself."

This Rocky guy growled. "You'll get your money when I say you do. And I can't give you something I haven't got yet." A pause. God, she wished she could see!

His voice went back to normal. "Don't worry, Jameson. You've proven yourself to the syndicate. I'll get you in, buddy."

Footsteps against the concrete told Josie her ally was gone. That left her there, trembling at the voice that had haunted her for months.

"Well, let's see if he got it right, sweet cheeks."

Ugh. She'd *hated* that nickname.

The bag over her head ripped away, bringing her face to face with— "Brad? What are you doing here?"

JOSIE'S VOICE CAME OVER their headphones in the van. Ross had been kind enough to give them their own so they could hear what was going on. "Brad? What are you doing here?"

Finn's brows furrowed. She knew this guy? But not as a captor.

"Josie, honey, I got a new job."

"Somehow I doubt that."

Brad's sneer was audible through the mic. "When did you start talking back like this? I thought you'd be happy to see me."

"You *sold me* into *slavery*! What about that makes you think I'd ever want to see your pathetic face again?"

She cried out as the unmistakable sound of a slap cracked through his headphones. Finn started to get up, but Roger threw an arm over his chest and held him down. He shook his head at him, but Finn vibrated with rage.

This was the ex that had betrayed her. Finn wanted his head.

"Now, we don't have anywhere to be for a few hours. Why don't we have one more roll in the hay, for old time's sake?" Finn broke out in a cold sweat at this sleazeball's tone. "No one said I couldn't sample the merchandise."

He swore he heard a molar crack as he clenched his jaw. "No!" Josie screamed.

It reminded him too much of that nightmare he'd interrupted. How many times had she screamed "no" only to be forced?

Roger's arm strained against him as he fought to get to her. He barely registered that Brad had removed the rope from her wrists. "We don't need this right now." The sound of nails scratching at skin echoed down the line. "Ow! You bitch!"

Good. Fight, Sunshine. Give him hell.

"Let me go!"

Ross was anything but passive in his chair. He was sending messages to the other agents. "Get in position for Plan Beta."

"What's Plan Beta?" Roger asked.

But Ross didn't have the chance to answer. "What the *hell* is this? You're wearing a wire!? Who's listening, Josephine?" Brad's screaming echoed in the warehouse.

Ross leaped from the van's backdoor. Roger and Finn tore off their earpieces and followed. Agents in body armor had gathered and closed in on the building.

Bang! Bang! Bang! "FBI!" With that, the agents at the building kicked in the door.

More agents lay in wait on the ridge overlooking the warehouse. Roger turned to Ross. "What's Plan Beta?" Thank God for his brother. Roger radiated true calm while Finn vibrated with barely suppressed tension. His Marine training was the only thing keeping him from going down there himself.

"Sniper. Hopefully, we can take him in, but if he dies, let God sort his ass." While Ross barked orders, Finn sidled over to where a sniper's stock, holding a rifle and scope, stood on the ground in front of the building, hidden by an evergreen bush.

A man around Finn's age lay in front of it. "Who the hell are you?"

"Finley Hunt, former Marine Corps." He leaned against a thick tree trunk and nodded down to the warehouse. "That's my girl in there."

"Shit, man. I'd be going even more crazy in your shoes." He laughed nervously. "Agent Robert Villa."

Finn took a long, assessing look at the man in front of him. His face was pale and sweat beaded his brow, despite the winter chill. "You been doing this long?"

"First assignment since I left the Rangers."

"I just got discharged myself about a month ago."

The agents that had gone in shuffled back out as Josie appeared in the doorway. Her clothes and hair were mussed, her body stiff as a board.

A dark-haired skinny guy trying to look tough in a leather jacket appeared behind her. He pulled something from behind Josie's back and pointed it at her head.

"We're walking out of here."

That coward! He was using her as a human shield. Finn snarled as he clenched his fists.

"Shit," Villa muttered. Finn glanced down to see him trembling.

"You with me, man?"

"She's too close. Not again." His voice was so quiet, Finn barely heard him. Dropping to his knees while the asshole ex was occupied talking to Ross, he checked in with Villa. He'd clean the bionic arm later.

"You here, man?"

"Fuck." Villa tore his hands away from the rifle and laid them on the ground. "I can't do it." It was obvious something was going wrong.

"What happened?" he whispered.

"The insurgent's holding a girl up in front of him and I can't get the shot!"

Glassy eyes told Finn Villa was no longer there with them. Flashbacks often came without warning, but this was something he should have informed his superiors about.

Finn opened his mouth before he could think about it for too long. "Let me do it."

"Sure, man. Just don't tell my CO."

"No worries. I got your six." Finn got himself situated in a flash, quickly familiarizing himself with the scope. Being behind the rifle again instantly calmed his nerves.

They'd need Brad for questioning, so Finn knew he'd better wound him. As satisfying as it would be to kill Josie's abusive ex, he didn't have the safety net following orders afforded him.

He looked down the scope at the asshole who had Josie hostage.

I'm coming for you, baby. Hold on.

JOSIE HADN'T EVEN HAD to use her code word before Ross had pulled the plug on this operation. And thank God he had. Brad had lost his mind when he saw the wire, changing his desire to rape her to a desire to kill her. For now, she was serving the purpose of his bargaining chip. If he got away, she knew she'd be dead before they found her.

Ross's voice called out from the wooded hill. "Release your hostage."

"Fat chance!" Brad spit on the ground. "You're my ticket to freedom, baby. And then we can talk about the company you've been keeping."

She shied away from him, but he held firm. That screaming session inside had reminded her of the first night he hit her. Over a guy in her group project, of all things.

I have to do this to graduate! It's not like that!

She could feel the hit she'd taken that night as if it had just happened. But he had barely touched her today.

"We can talk about this if you put your gun down and release the hostage."

"Fuck you!"

Brad's gun pushed against her skull, and she turned her head away. There, on the hill, she could make out the faint outline of the muzzle of a gun. A sniper? But Brad was holding her too close. They were the exact same height, so she was a rather effective human shield. And since he was looking in the wrong direction, he wouldn't see it.

While he rambled about how important he thought he was, she thought of Finn. She wanted to go to sleep in his arms again. To cook with him, make love to him, everything. She wanted everything with that sweet, intense man who asked too much of himself. He'd given her body back to her. Shown her pleasure beyond her wildest dreams and given her control over her own destiny. He supported her goals.

She loved him. And if Brad got her away from here, she'd never get to tell him!

Vaguely aware that Ross was trying to negotiate her release, she scanned the hillside, wishing she could see Finn one last time. Movement at the rifle obscured by the weeds drew her eye. A slow blinking light, cycling through red and green, reflected onto the tree she could only see from her angle. Finn had never changed the light on his arm after Christmas. Finn was behind the rifle!

She licked her lips, staring at where she thought the rifle was. Praying the scope let him see her message, since she didn't dare make a sound. If she died in the process, so be it. This time with Finn had been the best of her life. She'd go willingly if that meant the captives were free.

Do it, Finn, she mouthed. *I love you.*

She angled herself as far away from Brad as she could, and he snapped, wrapping his arm around her shoulders tighter. "Where do you think you're going?"

"Heaven."

A gun went off, and then another. Brad's arm dropped from her shoulders, and she fell to her knees on the gravel. The last thing she heard was Finn screaming her name as she lost consciousness.

Chapter 26

THE CLOSEST AGENT TO Josie caught her before she hit her head, laying her down on the ground while the other agents cuffed her ex. But Finn only had eyes for her.

He ran down the hill and fell to his knees, ignoring the bite of the gravel through his jeans. "Josie? Wake up, Sunshine!" Tears burned his eyes as he looked for a wound, the paramedics rushing over. "Baby, please."

Strong arms banded under his arms and dragged him away. Finn started to fight, but relaxed when he heard Roger's voice. "Easy, little bro. Let the medics do their job."

His chest heaved, watching the emergency responders check on his girl. Only Roger's hold kept him back.

"Get it out of your system, Finn."

"He shot…"

"That was Ross." Roger's words started to calm Finn's breathing. "He drew the bastard's fire to protect Josie."

His mind raced. "Then why…"

"No idea. But she wasn't shot."

Those paramedics finished their examination and went to help the ones attending to Brad. They had already cut Brad's coat off him and were packing the wound to stop the bleeding. Blood spray decorated the gravel at their feet, but they did their jobs.

"Josie…" She still hadn't woken up. He needed to hold her. But for now, he watched her chest rise and fall. She was alive.

Ross's voice was gentle. When had he walked over? "Let the medics stop the bleeding so we can haul him away. They might want to take her up on a gurney as well, I don't know."

Once Brad had been taken into custody, one of the paramedics walked over, snapping his gloves off. "She's okay. We believe she just fainted. Once she's awake, she may need treated for shock." He tucked the gloves into a back pocket. "But you can go to her now." Roger released him, and Finn closed the distance between them. He sat next to Josie and gently lifted her into his lap, curling his arms around her. The female agent she'd gone with barely an hour ago approached.

"Can I get the wire and the tracker off her?"

Looking around, none of the other agents were standing there anymore. He nodded, holding her as Agent Horne lifted her sweater, plucking the transmitter and microphone out of her bra. Afterward, she fixed Josie's clothes. Reaching behind Josie's ear, she pulled off what looked like a sticker. "Thank you. You were amazing." She smiled at them, a gesture she didn't seem to use much. Finn nodded again, just as the paramedics returned with another gurney.

"We've got the other guy situated. Let's get your girl up the hill."

"Finn?" Josie's hand reached up and patted his chest. "What happened?"

His sob broke free and Finn clutched her tighter. "You're okay!"

"Ma'am?" The paramedic looked down. "You fainted. Are you able to walk?"

"I-I think so." Finn rose with her, keeping his hands on her waist.

"Any dizziness?"

"No… a little woozy, maybe."

"Would you rather ride the gurney up? We don't want you to fall."

"Okay."

They strapped her in and Finn followed right behind, unable to take his eyes off her for a moment. When they reached the dirt road where all the vehicles were parked, the paramedics unbuckled her and Finn helped her into the van. Roger sat up front with Ross, so Finn slid across and buckled himself right next to Josie, unwilling to give her any space.

"You took ten years off my life, Sunshine." He cupped her face and pressed his lips to hers fervently, just to prove to himself that she was alive and well.

"You were awesome." Ross said as he pulled the van around to return to the office building where they'd left Roger's truck.

Josie laid her head on his shoulder, and Finn finally took a deep breath. "What happened to Brad?"

"We got him in the shoulder. He's cuffed and on his way to jail after the hospital." She let out a shuddering breath at Ross's words, and Finn kissed her forehead.

"I thought that was you?"

Finn shook his head, putting a finger to his lips. He wouldn't blow Villa's cover.

Ross dropped his chin to his chest, a grimace on his face. "I'm so sorry, Josie. I had no idea the contact was your ex."

She shivered, and Finn rubbed her arm. He remembered the words of the paramedic, that she might go into shock. "I thought he was still in Montana."

"You were amazing." Finn clenched his jaw at the red mark on her cheek. "So brave, baby." He tucked a piece of her hair behind her ear. Finn only wished he'd gotten five minutes alone with the man that had made his Sunshine suffer.

He'd have liked to even the score.

"What about the girls? The whole plan is a failure. I failed them." Tears ran down her face as she trembled next to him.

"Shh, no, sweetheart. The FBI has Brad, and they'll get the information out of him."

Ross nodded and backed Finn up. "Just as soon as he's awake. I think the little pussy passed out from the pain."

When they returned to the FBI building, the four of them went inside. Ross had them sign some forms before they were free to go. Then Roger, Finn, and Josie piled into the Silverado and headed out.

"Anyone hungry?" Roger asked. "We missed dinner."

"I could eat," Finn answered. He knew Josie had barely eaten all day, probably due to nerves.

Her stomach answered for her. "Starving."

"I'll hit the drive-thru," Roger said, turning the wheel toward a Checker's sign. "Dinner's on me."

They returned home with a bag full of food, with Josie slurping on her strawberry milkshake. Jenna, Sam, and Frankie met them at the door.

"Josie!" Frankie engulfed her in a hug.

"What are you guys doing here?"

"Jenna was worried and stressing me out over text, so we came over to keep her company."

"I brought the Switch and some games," Sam added. He nodded at Finn as he helped Roger carry the food into the dining room.

"Did you get my shake?" Jenna greeted her boyfriend with a kiss.

"Yes, Princess. One chocolate shake." He handed over the Styrofoam cup. "And one birthday cake for Frankie."

"Mmm mm, thanks, Roger." Frankie took a loud slurp and waggled her brows at Sam, who just shook his head.

"Francesca..."

"What? It's like vanilla with a little extra." She bumped her hip into his as she took her seat.

Over burgers and fries, Finn let Josie tell the group as much as she wanted about the ordeal. Which, as it turned out, was everything.

"The important thing is, he's behind bars, and hopefully, he'll sing like a canary." Jenna popped a few fries into her mouth.

"How'd you convince them to let you be the sniper, Finn?"

Finn shrugged. "Their sniper had a flashback, and couldn't do it, so I stepped in." He turned to her. "You moved your head at the perfect angle. Gave me the window I needed."

"Window? More like the eye of a needle." Roger took a sip of his beer. "I was watching, and she only moved her head an inch or so."

"He was holding so tightly it was all I could do."

"And it was perfect, sweetheart." He wrapped an arm around her shoulders and kissed her temple. Listening to her tell the story had his heart pumping again, and he needed to reassure himself she was okay. "But this information does not leave this room. Officially, their man pulled the trigger. Ross can't know it was me, or we'd be in a world of trouble."

Sam chuckled. "Good thing I quit working there."

All the energy drained out of her as she laid her head on his shoulder. Her food wrappers lay on the table.

"I'm exhausted."

"Well, it is ten o'clock." Jenna balled up the trash.

Frankie stood to help her. "We should get going, Sam."

"Thanks for dinner, Roger." Sam stood and gave Roger a back slapping hug, then clapped Finn on the shoulder. "Nice to see you again."

"You, too."

The girls hugged their goodbyes, and Finn took Josie's hand as he pulled her upstairs. "Come on, Sunshine."

"Alright."

FINN INSISTED ON LETTING her use the shower first, and hanging out in the bathroom while she did. Josie was glad to wash the day away, shampooing her hair in record time. The haircut had helped in that regard.

He took his turn while she dried her hair. When he reentered her room in his lounge pants, her mouth watered. But she wanted to have a little fun first.

"So, boyfriend, huh?"

He froze, his eyes wide. "Uh, why else would they let me stay?"

She let her hips sway as she strode across the room. "You didn't think you should talk to me about that first?"

Finn looked away, scrubbing a hand over his hair. It had grown out from his military cut, long enough to give her something to tug on.

"Sorry, Josie. It just slipped out."

Josie slid her hands up his chest with a chuckle. "I'm not mad. It just surprised me, that's all."

"Whew!" Finn made a big deal of wiping pretend sweat from his forehead.

Smiling felt amazing after the crazy day she'd had. "Bring your moisturizer over. I'll do your massage."

"I think it's still on the nightstand." Finn walked over and picked up the half empty tube. "I should get more."

"Sit down." She followed him to the bed.

"Aren't you wearing pajamas for this?" His gaze caressed her form, barely hidden by the fluffy white towel.

"Why bother? You're going to want to take them off, anyway." She squeezed out the lotion and lifted his stump up where she could reach it, starting the massage they now did nightly.

"It's moving really well. We probably won't have to do this much longer." Her fingers caressed his arm after she'd finished the medically necessary stuff, moving up his bicep in that way that made him shiver.

"Josie…" Her fingers danced across his shoulders as she leaned forward, placing her breasts in his face. He leaned away. "Are you up to this?"

Slowly, she straddled his hips, lowering herself down to his lap, where his cock stood at attention, like the first time she'd helped him with his massage. She rubbed her hands over his head, the teddy bear fuzz tickling her palms. He closed his eyes and let out a sound that resembled a cat's purr.

"I was so scared. Not of dying. Of him." He opened his eyes to look at her and gave her time to speak. "I went right back to the night he first got angry with me. I'd said something about a group project I was working on, and there was a guy in the group. He flew off the handle." Those intense green eyes drew out all her truths. "It was the first time he hit me. I had to stop at the convenience store on the way to campus to buy concealer." His only response was to grip her hip tighter. "But I needed to stay so I could afford school. And he promised it wouldn't happen again."

"He lied."

Josie nodded, repeating Finn's words. "He lied. The night he betrayed me and the syndicate took me, I had just opened a bank account in my name only. I planned to leave him as soon as I got my first paycheck. I was applying to all these nursing jobs that had starting bonuses so I could get away. Instead, it got worse." She took a deep breath, realizing his cock had gone flaccid. "Sorry, I know this isn't sexy bedroom talk."

Finn shook his head. "Don't apologize. I want to know everything about you, Sunshine. The good, the bad, the stuff that makes me want to kill your ex and everyone that hurt you."

"It's a long list." Josie let out a shaky laugh.

"You got one of the best snipers in the Corps on your side."

"You'd be no good to me in jail."

"Find a jury to convict me." The challenging look he gave her made her heart flutter. He was serious. He'd kill for her.

"So, you're saying, if he hadn't been using me as a shield..."

"You bet your ass he would have been in the ground." Then he stroked her hair. "But I wouldn't want you to be that close to death. You're so vibrant."

"I am, now. Thanks to your family, and you." She wrapped her arms around his shoulders and leaned forward to kiss him. "I love you, Finn."

"About that." His grip stopped her in her tracks. "What the fuck was up with telling me when I got a scope aimed at you, baby?"

Josie bit her lip. "I didn't know if Brad would get the shot off. And I needed you to know."

Finn shook his head. "Rude. I couldn't say it back like that." He moved his hand up to her chin. "I love you, too. Be my girlfriend, Josie. I'll probably suck at it, since I've never done it before—"

"Trust me, you're already the best boyfriend I've ever had."

He angled his thumb over her lips. "I wasn't done yet."

She gave him a sheepish look.

"I was going to say your ex set your expectations too low. So since I can't be the best sniper in the world anymore, I'm going to be the best boyfriend in the world. And after you're ready for it, the best husband in the world."

Tears pricked behind her eyes. She'd marry him tomorrow if he kept talking like this.

"Those are my intentions, Josie. What do you say?"

"Yes!" She pressed forward and claimed his mouth with hers, pushing him backward onto the bed. His excitement pressed against her core again, and she pulled her towel off. "I need you."

His fingers slipped between her legs, sliding against her clit. "Put those tits in my face, baby. Let me get you ready." Leaning up, she did as he asked, and he loved all over her breasts with his mouth. Licking, sucking, nips here and there that made her squeal. Then his fingers slipped inside her, gliding through her desire, and she moaned. Her hips pushed back against his hand.

"More."

"Get my pants off."

She scrambled to get off him, pulling the lounge pants and boxer briefs down and off. Reaching for the drawer, she pulled out a condom and laid it on the bed.

"How do you want it?"

Josie thought about his question. She needed to be surrounded by him, smothered by his love. "Think you can get on top this time?"

Finn worked his jaw from side to side as he considered. "Put a pillow under my arm, and we can try it."

She opened the foil packet with her teeth, enjoying the sharp inhale he made as he stroked his length. Once she rolled the latex over his cock, they traded places on the bed. She pulled a pillow over to lay on her left side, under where his right arm would go.

He settled between her legs, carrying most of his weight on his left arm. Then he slowly lowered himself down to his elbows., the pillow taking the place of his right forearm.

"Okay?" she asked, breathless.

He stared and stared. "Perfect." With a little maneuvering, and her hand guiding him, he slid inside her. She locked her legs around him and he started to move. Everything was so intense at this angle. The eye contact. Their skin touching everywhere. Slow and steady, he made love to her. "I love you so much."

"I love you too, Josie." Her climax built gradually, eventually cresting like a wave on the shore, but it went on and on. Finn followed her with a gasp, shuddering inside her.

They lay together even as he slipped out of her, foreheads together, breathing each other in. And Josie knew she'd go through everything all over again, if this was where she'd end up.

Chapter 27

"Happy New Year!" Finn opened the door to Ross and a cute, curvy brunette waiting on Roger's porch.

"Come on in. Thanks for coming." He took their coats up to the now empty guest room he'd once occupied.

"Ross! Heather!" Jenna exclaimed. Ah, that must be Ross's girlfriend. When he returned to the first floor, the buffet of food was in full swing. Finn filled a plate from the dishes along the kitchen island. Pork, sauerkraut, and, of course, black-eyed peas.

Josie smiled at him from the table next to the last empty place. "I grabbed you a beer."

"Thanks, baby." He leaned over and kissed her cheek as he sat down.

Looking around the table, Ross and Heather, Roger and Jenna, Frankie and Sam, and then him and Josie. But someone was missing,

"Hey, Rog, wasn't Jon supposed to come?"

"He's running late. Hit traffic leaving work." Roger said around a mouthful of pork. "He'll be here soon."

Vibrations shook the table. "Ross!" Heather gave her boyfriend an indignant look. "You said you were off tonight."

"It's only on for important calls, sweetheart." He pulled out his phone and swore. "I'll keep it quick." He answered the phone as he slipped out into the living room. "Patterson."

Heather turned back to the group, her face flushed. "I'm so sorry."

"Hey, it's the nature of the business. We understand." Finn smirked as his brother tried to set her at ease.

Ross didn't stay away long. He returned to the dining room and slumped back in his chair.

"Ross, is everything okay?"

"No, it's not." He looked over at Josie. "You okay with me giving you an update on your case here?"

"They're my friends and my security team. It's fine."

"True, they'd find out, anyway." He ran a hand through his hair and leaned forward. "Our canary is dead."

"Dead?"

Ross clenched his jaw. "It looks like suicide, but I seriously doubt it. I think the syndicate had someone on the inside that knew he was talking to us. What information we managed to get was helpful, but not enough." Ross scrubbed a hand over his face. "My undercover guy is going to have to be super careful now, and find a new way into the syndicate. It's good that we got Brad into custody quickly, because we were able to control the narrative he sent to his boss there."

Josie's hand gripped Finn's thigh. He dropped his left hand and moved it to cover hers. She had a brave face on, but she was scared.

"What did you tell them, Ross?" she asked. Finn's chest warmed with how steady her voice was.

"That there was an accident, and you didn't make it." Ross shrugged. "But they found him anyway, so I don't know how useful that is. I recommend you change your name, at the very least."

Josie nodded. "How do I do that legally?"

"I'll get Roger the forms. And I'll take care of it personally, so the records won't get leaked." Ross shook his head. "I'm sorry that I don't have better news."

"I'm not sorry he's dead." Josie told him. "I just wish you had a location for the captives."

"He did tell us where he was planning to take you." Josie's shoulders stiffened. "I'm still waiting on the full report from that raid. They didn't find anyone, but there were hairs left behind and they're running them through forensics to see what we can get from them."

"Okay."

"We'll find them, Josie. And I won't rest until we do."

JONATHON PULLED HIS BRIGHT red Dodge Ram truck up behind Finn's white F-150. Traffic on the Beltway had been a nightmare as usual, and it was nearly midnight. He'd wanted to be at Roger's New Year's Eve party hours ago, but work had gotten away from him again.

He knocked on the door, and Roger opened it. "Just in time! The ball's about to drop!"

"Happy New Year, Jon!" Roger's girlfriend, a hot little redhead named Jenna, plopped a gold foil top hat on his head from her perch on the staircase and handed him a noisemaker. "We're all in the living room."

"How about a kiss at midnight, sweetheart?" He gave Jenna a wink. She just rolled her eyes while Roger gave him a death glare. It was way too much fun to rile him up.

Finn had his bionic arm around Josie. Sam hugged Frankie from behind. The former FBI cybercrime specialist might have had too much to drink, because he was eyeing Frankie's ass like it was a hot fudge sundae. Jon doubted he usually did that in public.

"Ross, this is my other brother. Jon, this is Ross. He used to work with Sam. This is his girlfriend, Heather."

"Nice to meet you." Yet another woman off the market and not available for him.

Fuck, Jon was lonely. Granted, he could walk into a bar and charm any woman he wanted into going home for the night, but it wasn't the same. He wanted what his brothers had. He'd never actually steal their girls, but he had to admit their taste was impeccable.

Everyone else at this party was coupled up and lovey-dovey. He thought he'd had that, once. But she disappeared. Ever since then, he'd built the reputation of a player. Love 'em and leave 'em. It was easier to protect his heart that way.

But it was getting old.

Roger offered him a beer, and they watched the show happening in Times Square. When the camera panned to the ball at the top of the building, the whole house chanted along with the people in New York.

"Ten… nine… eight… seven… six… five… four… three.. two… one! Happy New Year!"

As *Auld Lang Syne* played over the speakers, the couples surrounding Jon kissed each other. Finn had Josie bent back over his arm. Sam gripped Frankie's ample butt in both hands. Jenna had climbed Roger like a tree. Ross and Heather wrapped their arms around each other like some crazy Kama Sutra pose he'd probably seen online.

He was happy for them, really. But it hurt.

A light tap on his shoulder got his attention. "Happy New Year, Jon." Josie, shy scared Josie, who he'd had to stop flirting with even as a joke, stood on her tiptoes and bussed his cheek.

"Thanks, Josie." That she would do that, of all the girls, meant a lot. He'd never meant to scare her, and this clear sign of her trust made his chest warm and a genuine smile spread across his mouth.

"Happy New Year, Jon." Jenna took his other cheek. "Everybody get outside and start making noise!"

"Grab the pots and pans!" cried Frankie. Everyone snatched a piece of metal cookware from the coffee table and ran outside to ring in the new year.

As he helped make a racket with Roger's skillet and a spoon, Jon thought to himself, *It's time to come home.*

341

Epilogue

FINN LAID THE QUARTER down on Vasquez's headstone. Yeah, technically he hadn't been in her hospital room when she died, but since she never woke up from the attack, he was claiming it. Josie stood nearby, keeping the Arizona sun out of her face with a wide-brimmed hat and sunglasses.

"Saved the best for last," he chuckled. They'd driven all over the country visiting his unit's last resting places. Hartmann had been buried in Arlington, a quick day trip, but Nicholson, Grant, and Vasquez had been from all over the US. Josie loved visiting all the different areas of the country, and they'd taken their sweet time going from place to place, giving him plenty of time between graveside visits.

His girlfriend was so understanding whenever Finn got lost in thought. She knew he and Rosa Vasquez had been friends with benefits, and she didn't care.

"What do you think of the new arm?" He flexed the bionic prosthesis. "Technology is amazing, right? I can even shoot again." Finn dropped his head. "I wish you were here to see it. Although I got a girlfriend now." He looked over at Josie, her corn silk hair flowing in the breeze. "Eh, I think you'd like her. She kicks my ass when I need it, so you'd approve."

There really wasn't much else to say. And he wanted to get Josie out of the sun so her pale skin didn't burn. He wasn't used to worrying about sunscreen in February.

"You were a hell of a Marine, Vasquez. It was an honor to serve with you. Rest in peace, my friend."

LATER THAT SPRING...

After five grueling hours of testing, Josie burst through the double doors and welcomed the warmth of the spring sun on her face. She threw her head back as the breeze played with her hair. Finally, after months of studying, it was over.

"Hey, Sunshine." Finn grinned from where he leaned against a brick pillar. "I got your smoothie."

"Thanks, handsome." She took it from him with a grateful sigh and let the cool strawberry flavor wash away the stress.

"How do you think you did?"

"We'll know in ten days." She shrugged, but grinned. It had been long and arduous, but she was confident she'd passed.

"I have faith in you."

Once her name change paperwork had come from the government, she hadn't wasted time and registered for the next available session. She'd kept her first name, but changed the last one to Miller. If Finn had his way, she'd be changing it again. Either way, Josie was anxious to move on with her life. Finn had started working for Roger's company, and when he wasn't, he was with her.

At her last therapy session, she'd discussed her concerns with joining the rigorous schedule of a hospital. Her therapist had suggested looking for less stressful nursing jobs instead, such as a doctor's office or a school.

She had some interviews set up next week with a couple of different practices. Hopefully one would hire her so she and Finn could talk about their next steps. As grateful as she was for Roger and Jenna's kindness, she wanted them to have their own space.

"What's the plan now?" Finn helped her into the truck and leaned into the doorway.

"Honestly, I'm exhausted. I just want to go home and watch a movie or something."

He waggled his brows. "Or something?"

Laughing, she swatted his hands away. "I'm too tired!"

"Alright. You can rest first." He winked and walked around to his side of the truck.

Josie shook her head. The man was insatiable. They'd be making out during the movie, and once the credits rolled, he'd be on her. The new arm that made it possible for him to return to working out also opened more traditional positions to them. Not that she minded being on top. Having him under her control was hot.

But the test had really taken it out of her.

So much so that she fell asleep halfway through the movie, despite it being the superhero action flick she'd been meaning to see since it came out.

She awoke as the end credits rolled, Finn chuckling beneath her. Groaning, she sat up.

"This is why we need our own place. I always fall asleep when we watch movies on your laptop in bed."

"I don't mind. Your snoring is cute."

She smacked him on the shoulder, but there was no heat behind it. "I do not snore."

He placed his thumb and forefinger about a half inch apart. "Just a little." Finn ducked her next swing, holding up his hand. "I got you something while you were in the test."

Josie tilted her head to one side. "What is it?"

He slid his hand down to the side of the bed and lifted a plain black shopping bag. "I saw the costume store and took a look around."

"Costume? But Halloween is months away."

"Well, try it on. If you don't like it, we can get something else."

Josie peeked inside the bag and shook her head. "Sexy nurse?"

Finn gave her his shit-eating grin.

She sighed. "Was this a sex shop?"

He made a show of zipping his lips and throwing away the key.

Good thing she'd had a nap. Slipping off the bed, Josie sashayed into the bathroom to change. This goofball. He put on a stoic facade, but in reality, he was kinda crazy.

Crazy about me. She chuckled to herself. The costume was easy to put on, a tight zip-up mini dress, thigh-high red fishnet stockings, and a red G-string. And, of course, the classic old-fashioned nurse hat that no one had worn since before Josie was born.

She fluffed her hair and moved her breasts up in their bra, letting her small cleavage spill from the low neckline. When she reentered the bedroom, Finn had his shirt off and was laying flat on the bed. His laptop rested on the nightstand.

"Hello, nurse!" Finn's gaze caressed her from head to toe.

"Good evening," she greeted him. "What brings you in today?"

"Uh, you?" Finn's adorable confusion made her giggle. "Oh! You want to roleplay."

"Well, I thought that was why you bought this. Unless you're not into LARP in the bedroom."

"All my blood seems to have left my brain, nurse. I'm not thinking clearly."

"Let's see where the blood went, shall we?" Josie made a big deal of touching him everywhere but his cock. She even went so far as to remove his pants but only inspect his legs.

"I don't think it's there, nurse."

"Hmmm, you're right. But there's one more place we can look for it." She slowly pulled down his tented boxer briefs, her boyfriend vibrating with need. "There it is! Does it hurt?"

Finn nodded, making a pathetic humming noise. "Can you make it better, nurse?"

"I know just the treatment."

Enjoying her costume and her role, she crawled up the bed starting at his feet, giving him an eyeful of her breasts in the costume. When she reached his hips, she sat back up, and then reached up her skirt to pull her panties to the side. Her core was slick as she teased his tip, slowly sinking more and more, then finally sinking down on his shaft until she was so full of him. They groaned in unison, and then Josie ground her clit against his pelvic bone.

She'd gotten an implant, and now they didn't need condoms. Josie loved the feel of nothing between them. Finn's hands gripped her hips and silently begged her to move. She bounced on his dick, and her orgasm started to build.

"It doesn't seem to be working. I think you need a more intense treatment." She said with a sly smirk and started to unzip her dress further.

"Oh yes, that's so much better." Finn sat up beneath her, his knees popping up to help support her. Once her whole bra was visible, he reached in and pulled her breasts forward through the dress. Then his mouth was on her, sucking on one nipple while tugging the other. She cried out, her walls clutching at him. Then he started thrusting from the bottom, hitting that secret spot inside her that made her explode.

"Yes! Finn right there!" All pretenses flew away, and they were Finn and Josie once more. She screamed as she came, and he kept thrusting until his own orgasm spilled inside her. They slumped together as their breathing evened out.

"I love you, Sunshine." Finn breathed.

"I love you, too." Then she started to laugh.

"What's so funny?"

"Just that I was all worried about dating you because you were my patient. But you surprise me with *this*."

"I like your style of healing." Finn shrugged.

She gave him a soft peck on the lips. "You healed me, too."

He grinned and wagged his eyebrows again. "How about a shower?"

"Oh, my God! You're ridiculous!" She kissed him again, pulling away before he could turn this into another round. "Yes, let's shower."

"After that, I want to show you the houses I found online."

"Houses?"

Finn shrugged. "Don't you want kids?"

"Yes. Eventually." She laughed as she took off the silly costume and hung it up in their closet. The G-string went into the hamper.

He sidled up behind her, wrapping his arms around her and pulled her into his naked body before laying his chin on her shoulder. "What do you want in a house?"

Josie thought for a moment. "Well, we talked about three kids, so at least four bedrooms. I want our bathroom to have an en suite. And I want a fence, so I don't have to worry about the kids when they play outside."

"My brother is going to help me with the security system, so I don't think that will be a problem."

"How about you? What do you want?"

"I'd like a gym in the basement like Roger has. And a shed to store the lawn mower."

"Are we going to have a big yard?"

"If I have anything to say about it, we will. We'll need somewhere for me to teach the kids about LARPing while you work all day. Then they'll be tired and go to sleep early so I can spend time with you." He nuzzled into her neck and she giggled.

"How are we going to afford this? I don't even have a job yet."

He squeezed her tight. "I got money in the bank from the Marines. It makes more sense to put a down payment on a house than it does to rent an apartment."

Josie shook her head. "I want my name on it, too. I'm not just moving into a house you're paying for."

"Whatever you want, baby."

Whatever she wanted. She could have this amazing man, her dream job, *and* her picket fence. Sometimes Josie wondered what she'd done to deserve Finn. And then she remembered the hell she'd been through.

Worth it. She thought as she reentered the bathroom, with Finn hot on her heels.

Absolutely worth it.

WANT TO BE THE first to know when Jon's book is coming out? Sign up for my newsletter here, or at www.jasminec caldwell.com

Also By Jasmine

For a current list of my available titles, scan the QR code below:

Notes from Jasmine

I am so happy with the way this book turned out. I knew back when I started outlining the series and Thief's Bodyguard that Finn was going to lose his arm. But I didn't want to give it away, so I had to dance around the issue in book 2 where Judy got the call. I even went so far as to eliminate any mentions of Finn's injury in my teaser posts online.

I am quite familiar with the way real life doesn't always give us good surprises, nor are the bad ones at a convenient time.

Setting this at the holiday season was a happy accident. The holidays are a healing time for me and I loved bringing that into Josie and Finn's journey.

Thank you, dear readers, for your patience, as I did not get to release this book as early as I would have liked. Jon's book will be out sometime in 2025, as early as I can. This should be the final installment of the fight against the syndicate and it looks like it's going to be a doozy to write.

Thank you Maria, my critique partner and coach, for making sure this story wasn't too slow burn (originally they didn't even meet until Chapter 9!). So many thanks to my beta team for all your wonderful insight and comments (and threatening to leave your husband for Finn). Jenn, your edits were spot on and they really made everything click together perfectly. I can't wait to keep working with you in the future! Sarah Kil, thank you for not threatening to kill me when I took forever picking a model. And so many thanks to Roxana, who got this book proofread in record time. Thanks to my hubby for being so supportive and understanding when the words just won't stop flowing. Thanks to H.K. Darkwood for your awesome sprinting streams. And as always, thanks to Jenna Moreci, Abbie Emmons and Dale L. Roberts for the YouTube videos.

XOXO,

Jasmine

About the Author

I inherited my love of reading from my parents. As the daughter of two teachers, one of whom is also a librarian, I was the kid who walked out of the library with the maximum number of books each week, then walked back in the following week having read every single one. This would go on all summer long. When I could put pencil to paper, I started writing my own (terrible) kid's stories. Around age eight, I told my mom I wanted to be an author when I grew up, but she talked me out of it. She wanted me to have a stable career because of my poor health.

While I learned to manage my chronic condition through childhood, I also kept writing as a creative outlet. But when I grew up and turned my focus to my career, writing went by the wayside. The stories would not come again until quarantine in 2020 when trauma from the year before poured out of me in a cathartic story now known as *Roar for Me*. The decision to self-publish was an easy one. I consider each book its own work of art and I want to control not only what I write, but all the packaging, as well.

I write books I want to read. This means intelligent characters, happy-ever-afters, and no cheating. Adult contemporary romances with plenty of steam appeal to me the most. Music and pop culture are my biggest sources of inspiration. And I love to flip the script and surprise readers by putting a twist on their expectations.

Everyone deserves their own love story. I've always believed that. I want to develop a wide range of characters so everyone can relate to someone in one of my books. I especially love challenging gender expectations. And I hope my books will be an escape for readers, not just entertainment. When I'm not writing, I'm working in healthcare in my native Pittsburgh. Or you might find me crafting, baking sweet treats, or playing *Mario Kart* with my own nerdy love.